T0312424

SINISTER SPRING

AGATHA CHRISTIE

SINISTER SPRING

MURDER AND MYSTERY
FROM THE QUEEN OF CRIME

HarperCollins*Publishers*

HarperCollins*Publishers*
1 London Bridge Street,
London SE1 9GF
www.harpercollins.co.uk

HarperCollins*Publishers*
Macken House,
39/40 Mayor Street Upper,
Dublin 1
D01 C9W8

Published by HarperCollins*Publishers* 2023

5

Cover and endpaper design by Holly Macdonald
© HarperCollins*Publishers* Ltd 2023
Illustrations: Shutterstock.com

A catalogue record for this book is
available from the British Library

ISBN 978-0-00-847089-0

Printed and bound in the UK
using 100% renewable electricity at CPI Group (UK) Ltd

CONTENTS

INTRODUCTION

The Gunman

It was just before I was five years old that I first met fear. Nursie and I were primrosing one spring day. We had crossed the railway line and gone up Shiphay lane, picking primroses from the hedges, where they grew thickly. We turned in through an open gate and went on picking. Our basket was growing full when a voice shouted at us, angry and rough:

'Wot d'you think you're doing 'ere?'

He seemed to me a giant of a man, angry and red-faced.

Nursie said we were doing no harm, only primrosing.

'Trespassing, that's what you're at. Get out of it. If you're not out of that gate in one minute, I'll boil you alive, see?'

I tugged desperately at Nursie's hand as we went. Nursie could not go fast, and indeed did not try to do so. My fear mounted. When we were at last safely in the lane I almost collapsed with relief. I was white and sick, as Nursie suddenly noticed.

'Dearie,' she said gently, 'you didn't think he *meant* it, did you? Not to boil you or whatever it was?'

I nodded dumbly. I had visualised it. A great steaming cauldron on a fire, myself being thrust into it. My agonised screams. It was all deadly real to me.

Nursie talked soothingly. It was a way people had of

speaking. A kind of joke, as it were. Not a nice man, a very rude, unpleasant man, but he hadn't meant what he said. It was a joke.

It had been no joke to me, and even now when I go into a field a slight tremor goes down my spine. From that day to this I have never known so real a terror.

Yet in nightmares I never relived this particular experience. All children have nightmares, and I doubt if they are a result of nursemaids or others 'frightening' them, or of any happening in real life. My own particular nightmare centred round someone I called 'The Gunman'. I never read a story about anyone of the kind. I called him The Gunman because he carried a gun, not because I was frightened of his shooting me, or for any reason connected with the gun. The gun was part of his appearance, which seems to me now to have been that of a Frenchman in grey-blue uniform, powdered hair in a queue and a kind of three-cornered hat, and the gun was some old-fashioned kind of musket. It was his mere presence that was frightening. The dream would be quite ordinary—a tea-party, or a walk with various people, usually a mild festivity of some kind. Then suddenly a feeling of uneasiness would come. There was someone—someone *who ought not to be there*—a horrid feeling of fear: and then I would see him—sitting at the tea-table, walking along the beach, joining in the game. His pale blue eyes would meet mine, and I would wake up shrieking: 'The Gunman, the Gunman!'

'Miss Agatha had one of her gunman dreams last night,' Nursie would report in her placid voice.

'Why is he so frightening, darling?' my mother would ask. 'What do you think he will do to you?'

I didn't know why he was frightening. Later the dream varied. The Gunman was not always in costume.

Sometimes, as we sat round a tea-table, I would look across at a friend, or a member of the family, and I would suddenly realise that it was *not* Dorothy or Phyllis or Monty, or my mother or whoever it might be. The pale blue eyes in the familiar face met mine—under the familiar appearance. *It was really the Gunman.*

Agatha Christie

SINISTER SPRING

The Market Basing Mystery

'After all, there's nothing like the country, is there?' said Inspector Japp, breathing in heavily through his nose and out through his mouth in the most approved fashion.

Poirot and I applauded the sentiment heartily. It had been the Scotland Yard inspector's idea that we should all go for the weekend to the little country town of Market Basing. When off duty, Japp was an ardent botanist, and discoursed upon minute flowers possessed of unbelievably lengthy Latin names (somewhat strangely pronounced) with an enthusiasm even greater than that he gave to his cases.

'Nobody knows us, and we know nobody,' explained Japp. 'That's the idea.'

This was not to prove quite the case, however, for the local constable happened to have been transferred from a village fifteen miles away where a case of arsenical poisoning had brought him into contact with the Scotland Yard man. However, his delighted recognition of the great man only enhanced Japp's sense of well-being, and as we sat down to breakfast on Sunday morning in the parlour of the village inn, with the sun shining, and tendrils of honeysuckle thrusting themselves in at the window, we were all in the best of spirits. The bacon and eggs were excellent, the coffee not so good, but passable and boiling hot.

'This is the life,' said Japp. 'When I retire, I shall have a little place in the country. Far from crime, like this!'

'*Le crime, il est partout*,' remarked Poirot, helping himself to a neat square of bread, and frowning at a sparrow which had balanced itself impertinently on the windowsill.

I quoted lightly:

> 'That rabbit has a pleasant face,
> His private life is a disgrace
> I really could not tell to you
> The awful things that rabbits do.'

'Lord,' said Japp, stretching himself backward, 'I believe I could manage another egg, and perhaps a rasher or two of bacon. What do you say, Captain?'

'I'm with you,' I returned heartily. 'What about you, Poirot?'

Poirot shook his head.

'One must not so replenish the stomach that the brain refuses to function,' he remarked.

'I'll risk replenishing the stomach a bit more,' laughed Japp. 'I take a large size in stomachs; and by the way, you're getting stout yourself, M. Poirot. Here, miss, eggs and bacon twice.'

At that moment, however, an imposing form blocked the doorway. It was Constable Pollard.

'I hope you'll excuse me troubling the inspector, gentlemen, but I'd be glad of his advice.'

'I'm on holiday,' said Japp hastily. 'No work for me. What is the case?'

'Gentleman up at Leigh House—shot himself—through the head.'

'Well, they will do it,' said Japp prosaically. 'Debt, or a woman, I suppose. Sorry I can't help you, Pollard.'

'The point is,' said the constable, 'that he can't have shot himself. Leastways, that's what Dr Giles says.'

Japp put down his cup.

'*Can't* have shot himself? What do you mean?'

'That's what Dr Giles says,' repeated Pollard. 'He says it's plumb impossible. He's puzzled to death, the door being locked on the inside and the windows bolted; but he sticks to it that the man couldn't have committed suicide.'

That settled it. The further supply of bacon and eggs was waved aside, and a few minutes later we were all walking as fast as we could in the direction of Leigh House, Japp eagerly questioning the constable.

The name of the deceased was Walter Protheroe; he was a man of middle age and something of a recluse. He had come to Market Basing eight years ago and rented Leigh House, a rambling, dilapidated old mansion fast falling into ruin. He lived in a corner of it, his wants attended to by a housekeeper whom he had brought with him. Miss Clegg was her name, and she was a very superior woman and highly thought of in the village. Just lately Mr Protheroe had had visitors staying with him, a Mr and Mrs Parker from London. This morning, unable to get a reply when she went to call her master, and finding the door locked, Miss Clegg became alarmed, and telephoned for the police and the doctor. Constable Pollard and Dr Giles had arrived at the same moment. Their united efforts had succeeded in breaking down the oak door of his bedroom.

Mr Protheroe was lying on the floor, shot through the head, and the pistol was clasped in his right hand. It looked a clear case of suicide.

3

After examining the body, however, Dr Giles became clearly perplexed, and finally he drew the constable aside, and communicated his perplexities to him; whereupon Pollard had at once thought of Japp. Leaving the doctor in charge, he had hurried down to the inn.

By the time the constable's recital was over, we had arrived at Leigh House, a big, desolate house surrounded by an unkempt, weed-ridden garden. The front door was open, and we passed at once into the hall and from there into a small morning-room whence proceeded the sound of voices. Four people were in the room: a somewhat flashily dressed man with a shifty, unpleasant face to whom I took an immediate dislike; a woman of much the same type, though handsome in a coarse fashion; another woman dressed in neat black who stood apart from the rest, and whom I took to be the housekeeper; and a tall man dressed in sporting tweeds, with a clever, capable face, and who was clearly in command of the situation.

'Dr Giles,' said the constable, 'this is Detective-Inspector Japp of Scotland Yard, and his two friends.'

The doctor greeted us and made us known to Mr and Mrs Parker. Then we accompanied them upstairs. Pollard, in obedience to a sign from Japp, remained below, as it were on guard over the household. The doctor led us upstairs and along a passage. A door was open at the end; splinters hung from the hinges, and the door itself had crashed to the floor inside the room.

We went in. The body was still lying on the floor. Mr Protheroe had been a man of middle age, bearded, with hair grey at the temples. Japp went and knelt by the body.

'Why couldn't you leave it as you found it?' he grumbled.

4

The doctor shrugged his shoulders.

'We thought it a clear case of suicide.'

'H'm!' said Japp. 'Bullet entered the head behind the left ear.'

'Exactly,' said the doctor. 'Clearly impossible for him to have fired it himself. He'd have had to twist his hand right round his head. It couldn't have been done.'

'Yet you found the pistol clasped in his hand? Where is it, by the way?'

The doctor nodded to the table.

'But it wasn't clasped in his hand,' he said. 'It was inside the hand, but the fingers weren't closed over it.'

'Put there afterwards,' said Japp; 'that's clear enough.' He was examining the weapon. 'One cartridge fired. We'll test it for fingerprints, but I doubt if we'll find any but yours, Dr Giles. How long has he been dead?'

'Some time last night. I can't give the time to an hour or so, as those wonderful doctors in detective stories do. Roughly, he's been dead about twelve hours.'

So far, Poirot had not made a move of any kind. He had remained by my side, watching Japp at work and listening to his questions. Only, from time to time, he had sniffed the air very delicately, and as if puzzled. I too had sniffed, but could detect nothing to arouse interest. The air seemed perfectly fresh and devoid of odour. And yet, from time to time, Poirot continued to sniff it dubiously, as though his keener nose detected something I had missed.

Now, as Japp moved away from the body, Poirot knelt down by it. He took no interest in the wound. I thought at first that he was examining the fingers of the hand that had held the pistol, but in a minute I saw that it was a handkerchief carried in the coat-sleeve that interested him. Mr Protheroe was dressed in a dark grey lounge-suit. Finally Poirot got up from his knees, but his eyes still strayed back to the handkerchief as though puzzled.

Japp called to him to come and help to lift the door. Seizing my opportunity, I too knelt down, and taking the handkerchief from the sleeve, scrutinized it minutely. It was a perfectly plain handkerchief of white cambric; there was no mark or stain on it of any kind. I replaced it, shaking my head and confessing myself baffled.

The others had raised the door. I realized that they were hunting for the key. They looked in vain.

'That settles it,' said Japp. 'The window's shut and bolted. The murderer left by the door, locking it and taking the key with him. He thought it would be accepted that Protheroe had locked himself in and shot himself, and that the absence of the key would not be noticed. You agree, M. Poirot?'

'I agree, yes; but it would have been simpler and better to slip the key back inside the room under the door. Then it would look as though it had fallen from the lock.'

'Ah, well, you can't expect everybody to have the bright ideas that you have. You'd have been a holy terror if you'd taken to crime. Any remarks to make, M. Poirot?'

Poirot, it seemed to me, was somewhat at a loss. He looked round the room and remarked mildly and almost apologetically: 'He smoked a lot, this monsieur.'

True enough, the grate was filled with cigarette-stubs, as was an ashtray that stood on a small table near the big armchair.

'He must have got through about twenty cigarettes last night,' remarked Japp. Stooping down, he examined the contents of the grate carefully, then transferred his attention to the ashtray. 'They're all the same kind,' he announced, 'and smoked by the same man. There's nothing there, M. Poirot.'

'I did not suggest that there was,' murmured my friend.

'Ha,' cried Japp, 'what's this?' He pounced on something bright and glittering that lay on the floor near the dead man. 'A broken cuff-link. I wonder who this belongs to. Dr Giles, I'd be obliged if you'd go down and send up the housekeeper.'

'What about the Parkers? He's very anxious to leave the house—says he's got urgent business in London.'

'I dare say. It'll have to get on without him. By the way things are going, it's likely that there'll be some urgent business down here for him to attend to! Send up the housekeeper, and don't let either of the Parkers give you and Pollard the slip. Did any of the household come in here this morning?'

The doctor reflected.

'No, they stood outside in the corridor while Pollard and I came in.'

'Sure of that?'

'Absolutely certain.'

The doctor departed on his mission.

'Good man, that,' said Japp approvingly. 'Some of these sporting doctors are first-class fellows. Well, I wonder who shot this chap. It looks like one of the three in the house. I hardly suspect the housekeeper. She's had eight years to shoot him in if she wanted to. I wonder who these Parkers are? They're not a prepossessing-looking couple.'

Miss Clegg appeared at this juncture. She was a thin, gaunt woman with neat grey hair parted in the middle, very staid and calm in manner. Nevertheless there was an air of efficiency about her which commanded respect. In answer to Japp's questions, she explained that she had been with the dead man for fourteen years. He had been a generous and considerate master. She had never seen Mr and Mrs Parker until three days ago, when they arrived unexpectedly to stay. She was of the opinion that they had asked themselves—the master had certainly not seemed pleased to see them. The cuff-links which Japp showed her had not belonged to Mr Protheroe—she was sure of that. Questioned about the pistol, she said that she believed her master had a weapon of that kind. He kept it locked up. She had seen it once some years ago, but could not say whether this was the same one. She had heard no shot last night, but that was not surprising, as it was a big, rambling house, and her rooms and those prepared for the Parkers were at the other end of the building. She did not know what time Mr Protheroe had gone to bed—he was still up when she retired at half past nine. It was not his habit to go at once to bed when he went to his room. Usually he would sit up half the night, reading and smoking. He was a great smoker.

Then Poirot interposed a question:

'Did your master sleep with his window open or shut, as a rule?' Miss Clegg considered.

'It was usually open, at any rate at the top.'

'Yet now it is closed. Can you explain that?'

'No, unless he felt a draught and shut it.'

Japp asked her a few more questions and then dismissed her. Next he interviewed the Parkers separately. Mrs Parker was inclined to be hysterical and tearful; Mr Parker was full of bluster and abuse. He denied that the cuff-link was his, but as his wife had previously recognized it, this hardly improved matters for him; and as he had also denied ever having been in Protheroe's room, Japp considered that he had sufficient evidence to apply for a warrant.

Leaving Pollard in charge, Japp bustled back to the village and got into telephonic communication with headquarters. Poirot and I strolled back to the inn.

'You're unusually quiet,' I said. 'Doesn't the case interest you?'

'*Au contraire*, it interests me enormously. But it puzzles me also.'

'The motive is obscure,' I said thoughtfully, 'but I'm certain that Parker's a bad lot. The case against him seems pretty clear but for the lack of motive, and that may come out later.'

'Nothing struck you as being especially significant, although overlooked by Japp?'

I looked at him curiously.

'What have you got up your sleeve, Poirot?'

'What did the dead man have up his sleeve?'

'Oh, that handkerchief!'

'Exactly, that handkerchief.'

'A sailor carries his handkerchief in his sleeve,' I said thoughtfully.

'An excellent point, Hastings, though not the one I had in mind.'

'Anything else?'

'Yes, over and over again I go back to the smell of cigarette-smoke.'

'I didn't smell any,' I cried wonderingly.

'No more did I, *cher ami*.'

I looked earnestly at him. It is so difficult to know when Poirot is pulling one's leg, but he seemed thoroughly in earnest and was frowning to himself.

★　　★　　★

The inquest took place two days later. In the meantime other evidence had come to light. A tramp had admitted that he had climbed over the wall into the Leigh House garden, where he often slept in a shed that was left unlocked. He declared that at twelve o'clock he had heard two men quarrelling loudly in a room on the first floor. One was demanding a sum of money; the other was angrily refusing. Concealed behind a bush, he had seen the two men as they passed and repassed the lighted window. One he knew well as being Mr Protheroe, the owner of the house; the other he identified positively as Mr Parker.

It was clear now that the Parkers had come to Leigh House to blackmail Protheroe, and when later it was discovered that the dead man's real name was Wendover, and that he had been a lieutenant in the Navy and had been concerned in the blowing up of the first-class cruiser *Merrythought*, in 1910, the case seemed to be rapidly clearing. It was supposed that Parker, cognizant of the part Wendover had played, had tracked him down and demanded hush-money which the other refused to pay. In the course of the quarrel, Wendover drew his revolver, and Parker snatched it from him and shot him, subsequently endeavouring to give it the appearance of suicide.

Parker was committed for trial, reserving his defence. We had attended the police-court proceedings. As we left, Poirot nodded his head.

'It must be so,' he murmured to himself. 'Yes, it must be so. I will delay no longer.'

He went into the post office, and wrote off a note which he despatched by special messenger. I did not see to whom it was addressed. Then we returned to the inn where we had stayed on that memorable weekend.

Poirot was restless, going to and from the window.

'I await a visitor,' he explained. 'It cannot be—surely it cannot be that I am mistaken? No, here she is.'

To my utter astonishment, in another minute Miss Clegg walked into the room. She was less calm than usual, and was breathing hard as though she had been running. I saw the fear in her eyes as she looked at Poirot.

'Sit down, mademoiselle,' he said kindly. 'I guessed rightly, did I not?'

For answer she burst into tears.

'Why did you do it?' asked Poirot gently. 'Why?'

'I loved him so,' she answered. 'I was nursemaid to him when he was a little boy. Oh, be merciful to me!'

'I will do all I can. But you understand that I cannot permit an innocent man to hang—even though he is an unpleasing scoundrel.'

She sat up and said in a low voice: 'Perhaps in the end I could not have, either. Do whatever must be done.'

Then, rising, she hurried from the room.

'Did she shoot him?' I asked utterly bewildered. Poirot smiled and shook his head.

'He shot himself. Do you remember that he carried his handkerchief in his *right* sleeve? That showed me that he was left-handed. Fearing exposure, after his stormy interview with Mr Parker, he shot himself. In the morning Miss Clegg came to call him as usual and found him lying dead. As she has just told us, she had known him from a little boy upward, and was filled with fury against the Parkers, who had driven him to this shameful death. She regarded them as murderers, and then suddenly she saw a chance of making them suffer for the deed they had inspired. She alone knew that he was left-handed. She changed the pistol to his right hand, closed and bolted the window, dropped the bit of cuff-link she had picked up in one of the downstairs rooms, and went out, locking the door and removing the key.'

'Poirot,' I said, in a burst of enthusiasm, 'you are magnificent. All that from the one little clue of the handkerchief.'

'And the cigarette-smoke. If the window had been closed, and all those cigarettes smoked, the room ought to have been full of stale tobacco. Instead, it was perfectly fresh, so I deduced at once that the window must have been open all night, and only closed in the morning, and that gave me a very interesting line of speculation. I could conceive of no circumstances under which a murderer could want to shut the window. It would be to his advantage to leave it open, and pretend that the murderer had escaped that way, if the theory of suicide did not go down. Of course, the tramp's evidence, when I heard it, confirmed my suspicions. He could never have overheard that conversation unless the window had been open.'

'Splendid!' I said heartily. 'Now, what about some tea?'

'Spoken like a true Englishman,' said Poirot with a sigh. 'I suppose it is not likely that I could obtain here a glass of *sirop*?'

The Case of the Missing Lady

The buzzer on Mr Blunt's desk—International Detective Agency, Manager, Theodore Blunt—uttered its warning call. Tommy and Tuppence both flew to their respective peepholes which commanded a view of the outer office. There it was Albert's business to delay the prospective client with various artistic devices.

'I will see, sir,' he was saying. 'But I'm afraid Mr Blunt is very busy just at present. He is engaged with Scotland Yard on the phone just now.'

'I'll wait,' said the visitor. 'I haven't got a card with me, but my name is Gabriel Stavansson.'

The client was a magnificent specimen of manhood, standing over six foot high. His face was bronzed and weatherbeaten, and the extraordinary blue of his eyes made an almost startling contrast to the brown skin.

Tommy swiftly made up his mind. He put on his hat, picked up some gloves and opened the door. He paused on the threshold.

'This gentleman is waiting to see you, Mr Blunt,' said Albert.

A quick frown passed over Tommy's face. He took out his watch.

'I am due at the Duke's at a quarter to eleven,' he said. Then he looked keenly at the visitor. 'I can give you a few minutes if you will come this way.'

The latter followed him obediently into the inner office, where Tuppence was sitting demurely with pad and pencil.

'My confidential secretary, Miss Robinson,' said Tommy. 'Now, sir, perhaps you will state your business? Beyond the fact that it is urgent, that you came here in a taxi, and that you have lately been in the Arctic—or possibly the Antarctic, I know nothing.'

The visitor stared at him in amazement.

'But this is marvellous,' he cried. 'I thought detectives only did such things in books! Your office boy did not even give you my name!'

Tommy sighed deprecatingly.

'Tut, tut, all that was very easy,' he said. 'The rays of the midnight sun within the Arctic circle have a peculiar action upon the skin—the actinic rays have certain properties. I am writing a little monograph on the subject shortly. But all this is wide of the point. What is it that has brought you to me in such distress of mind?'

'To begin with, Mr Blunt, my name is Gabriel Stavansson—'

'Ah! of course,' said Tommy. 'The well-known explorer. You have recently returned from the region of the North Pole, I believe?'

'I landed in England three days ago. A friend who was cruising in northern waters brought me back on his yacht. Otherwise I should not have got back for another fortnight. Now I must tell you, Mr Blunt, that before I started on this last expedition two years ago, I had the great good fortune to become engaged to Mrs Maurice Leigh Gordon—'

Tommy interrupted.

'Mrs Leigh Gordon was, before her marriage—?'

'The Honourable Hermione Crane, second daughter of Lord Lanchester,' reeled off Tuppence glibly.

Tommy threw her a glance of admiration.

'Her first husband was killed in the war,' added Tuppence.

Gabriel Stavansson nodded.

'That is quite correct. As I was saying, Hermione and I became engaged. I offered, of course, to give up this expedition, but she wouldn't hear of such a thing—bless her! She's the right kind of woman for an explorer's wife. Well, my first thought on landing was to see Hermione. I sent a telegram from Southampton, and rushed up to town by the first train. I knew that she was living for the time being with an aunt of hers, Lady Susan Clonray, in Pont Street, and I went straight there. To my great disappointment, I found that Hermy was away visiting some friends in Northumberland. Lady Susan was quite nice about it, after getting over her first surprise at seeing me. As I told you, I wasn't expected for another fortnight. She said Hermy would be returning in a few days' time. Then I asked for her address, but the old woman hummed and hawed—said Hermy was staying at one or two different places and that she wasn't quite sure what order she was taking them in. I may as well tell you, Mr Blunt, that Lady Susan and I have never got on very well. She's one of those fat women with double chins. I loathe fat women—always have— fat women and fat dogs are an abomination unto the Lord—and unfortunately they so often go together! It's an idiosyncrasy of mine, I know—but there it is—I never can get on with a fat woman.'

'Fashion agrees with you, Mr Stavansson,' said Tommy dryly. 'And every one has their own pet aversion—that of the late Lord Roberts was cats.'

'Mind you, I'm not saying that Lady Susan isn't a perfectly charming woman—she may be, but I've never taken to her. I've always felt, deep down, that she disapproved of our engagement, and I feel sure that she would influence Hermy against me if that were possible. I'm telling you this for what it's worth. Count it out as prejudice if you like. Well, to go on with my story, I'm the kind of obstinate brute who likes his own way. I didn't leave Pont Street until I'd got out of her the names and addresses of the people Hermy was likely to be staying with. Then I took the mail train north.'

'You are, I perceive, a man of action, Mr Stavansson,' said Tommy, smiling.

'The thing came upon me like a bombshell. Mr Blunt, none of these people had seen a sign of Hermy. Of the three houses, only one had been expecting her— Lady Susan must have made a bloomer over the other two—and she had put off her visit there at the last moment by telegram. I returned post haste to London, of course, and went straight to Lady Susan. I will do her the justice to say that she seemed upset. She admitted that she had no idea where Hermy could be. All the same, she strongly negatived any idea of going to the police. She pointed out that Hermy was not a silly young girl, but an independent woman who had always been in the habit of making her own plans. She was probably carrying out some idea of her own.

'I thought it quite likely that Hermy didn't want to report all her movements to Lady Susan. But I was still worried. I had that queer feeling one gets when something is wrong. I was just leaving when a telegram was brought to Lady Susan. She read it with an expression of relief and handed it to me. It ran as follows: "*Changed my plans. Just off to Monte Carlo for a week. —Hermy*".'

Tommy held out his hand.

'You have got the telegram with you?'

'No, I haven't. But it was handed in at Maldon, Surrey. I noticed that at the time, because it struck me as odd. What should Hermy be doing at Maldon. She'd no friends there that I had ever heard of.'

'You didn't think of rushing off to Monte Carlo in the same way that you had rushed north?'

'I thought of it, of course. But I decided against it. You see, Mr Blunt, whilst Lady Susan seemed quite satisfied by that telegram, I wasn't. It struck me as odd that she should always telegraph, not write. A line or two in her own handwriting would have set all my fears at rest. But anyone can sign a telegram "Hermy." The more I thought it over, the more uneasy I got. In the end I went down to Maldon. That was yesterday afternoon. It's a fair-sized place—good links there and all that—two hotels. I inquired everywhere I could think of, but there wasn't a sign that Hermy had ever been there. Coming back in the train I read your advertisement and I thought I'd put it up to you. If Hermy has really gone off to Monte Carlo, I don't want to set the police on her track and make a scandal, but I'm not going to be sent off on a wild goose chase myself. I stay here in London, in case—in case there's been foul play of any kind.'

Tommy nodded thoughtfully.

'What do you suspect exactly?'

'I don't know. But I feel there's something wrong.'

With a quick movement, Stavansson took a case from his pocket and laid it open before them.

'That is Hermione,' he said. 'I will leave it with you.'

The photograph represented a tall, willowy woman, no longer in her first youth, but with a charming frank smile and lovely eyes.

17

'Now, Mr Stavansson,' said Tommy, 'there is nothing you have omitted to tell me?'

'Nothing whatsoever.'

'No detail, however small?'

'I don't think so.'

Tommy sighed.

'That makes the task harder,' he observed. 'You must often have noticed, Mr Stavansson, in reading of crime, how one small detail is all the great detective needs to set him on the track. I may say that this case presents some unusual features. I have, I think, partially solved it already, but time will show.'

He picked up a violin which lay on the table and drew the bow once or twice across the strings. Tuppence ground her teeth, and even the explorer blenched. The performer laid the instrument down again.

'A few chords from Mosgovskensky,' he murmured. 'Leave me your address, Mr Stavansson, and I will report progress to you.'

As the visitor left the office, Tuppence grabbed the violin, and putting it in the cupboard turned the key in the lock.

'If you must be Sherlock Holmes,' she observed, 'I'll get you a nice little syringe and a bottle labelled cocaine, but for God's sake leave that violin alone. If that nice explorer man hadn't been as simple as a child, he'd have seen through you. Are you going on with the Sherlock Holmes touch?'

'I flatter myself that I have carried it through very well so far,' said Tommy with some complacence. 'The deductions were good, weren't they? I had to risk the taxi. After all, it's the only sensible way of getting to this place.'

'It's lucky I had just read the bit about his engagement in this morning's *Daily Mirror*,' remarked Tuppence.

'Yes, that looked well for the efficiency of Blunt's Brilliant Detectives. This is decidedly a Sherlock Holmes case. Even you cannot have failed to notice the similarity between it and the disappearance of Lady Frances Carfax.'

'Do you expect to find Mrs Leigh Gordon's body in a coffin?'

'Logically, history should repeat itself. Actually— well, what do you think?'

'Well,' said Tuppence. 'The most obvious explanation seems to be that for some reason or other, Hermy, as he calls her, is afraid to meet her fiancé, and that Lady Susan is backing her up. In fact, to put it bluntly, she's come a cropper of some kind, and has got the wind up about it.'

'That occurred to me also,' said Tommy. 'But I thought we'd better make pretty certain before suggesting that explanation to a man like Stavansson. What about a run down to Maldon, old thing? And it would do no harm to take some golf clubs with us.'

Tuppence agreeing, the International Detective Agency was left in the charge of Albert.

Maldon, though a well-known residential place, did not cover a large area. Tommy and Tuppence, making every possible inquiry that ingenuity could suggest, nevertheless drew a complete blank. It was as they were returning to London that a brilliant idea occurred to Tuppence.

'Tommy, why did they put Maldon, Surrey, on the telegram?'

'Because Maldon is in Surrey, idiot.'

'Idiot yourself—I don't mean that. If you get a telegram from—Hastings, say, or Torquay, they don't put the county after it. But from Richmond, they do put Richmond, Surrey. That's because there are two Richmonds.'

Tommy, who was driving, slowed up.

'Tuppence,' he said affectionately, 'your idea is not so dusty. Let us make inquiries at yonder post office.'

They drew up before a small building in the middle of a village street. A very few minutes sufficed to elicit the information that there were two Maldons. Maldon, Surrey, and Maldon, Sussex, the latter, a tiny hamlet but possessed of a telegraph office.

'That's it,' said Tuppence excitedly. 'Stavansson knew Maldon was in Surrey, so he hardly looked at the word beginning with S after Maldon.'

'Tomorrow,' said Tommy, 'we'll have a look at Maldon, Sussex.'

Maldon, Sussex, was a very different proposition to its Surrey name-sake. It was four miles from a railway station, possessed two public houses, two small shops, a post and telegraph office combined with a sweet and picture postcard business, and about seven small cottages. Tuppence took on the shops whilst Tommy betook himself to the Cock and Sparrow. They met half an hour later.

'Well?' said Tuppence.

'Quite good beer,' said Tommy, 'but no information.'

'You'd better try the King's Head,' said Tuppence. 'I'm going back to the post office. There's a sour old woman there, but I heard them yell to her that dinner was ready.'

She returned to the place and began examining post-cards. A fresh-faced girl, still munching, came out of the back room.

'I'd like these, please,' said Tuppence. 'And do you mind waiting whilst I just look over these comic ones?'

She sorted through a packet, talking as she did so.

'I'm ever so disappointed you couldn't tell me my sister's address. She's staying near here and I've lost her letter. Leigh Gordon, her name is.'

The girl shook her head.

'I don't remember it. And we don't get many letters through here either—so I probably should if I'd seen it on a letter. Apart from the Grange, there isn't many big houses round about.'

'What is the Grange?' asked Tuppence. 'Who does it belong to?'

'Dr Horriston has it. It's turned into a nursing home now. Nerve cases mostly, I believe. Ladies that come down for rest cures, and all that sort of thing. Well, it's quiet enough down here, heaven knows.' She giggled.

Tuppence hastily selected a few cards and paid for them.

'That's Doctor Horriston's car coming along now,' exclaimed the girl.

Tuppence hurried to the shop door. A small two-seater was passing. At the wheel was a tall dark man with a neat black beard and a powerful unpleasant face. The car went straight on down the street. Tuppence saw Tommy crossing the road towards her.

'Tommy, I believe I've got it. Doctor Horriston's nursing home.'

'I heard about it at the King's Head, and I thought there might be something in it. But if she's had a nervous breakdown or anything of that sort, her aunt and her friends would know about it surely.'

'Ye-es. I didn't mean that. Tommy, did you see that man in the two-seater?'

'Unpleasant-looking brute, yes.'

'That was Doctor Horriston.'

Tommy whistled.

'Shifty looking beggar. What do you say about it, Tuppence? Shall we go and have a look at the Grange?'

They found the place at last, a big rambling house, surrounded by deserted grounds, with a swift mill stream running behind the house.

'Dismal sort of abode,' said Tommy. 'It gives me the creeps, Tuppence. You know, I've a feeling this is going to turn out a far more serious matter than we thought at first.'

'Oh, don't. If only we are in time. That woman's in some awful danger; I feel it in my bones.'

'Don't let your imagination run away with you.'

'I can't help it. I mistrust that man. What shall we do? I think it would be a good plan if I went and rang the bell alone first and asked boldly for Mrs Leigh Gordon just to see what answer I get. Because, after all, it may be perfectly fair and above board.'

Tuppence carried out her plan. The door was opened almost immediately by a manservant with an impassive face.

'I want to see Mrs Leigh Gordon, if she is well enough to see me.'

She fancied that there was a momentary flicker of the man's eyelashes, but he answered readily enough.

'There is no one of that name here, madam.'

'Oh, surely. This is Doctor Horriston's place, The Grange, is it not?'

'Yes, madam, but there is nobody of the name of Mrs Leigh Gordon here.'

Baffled, Tuppence was forced to withdraw and hold a further consultation with Tommy outside the gate.

'Perhaps he was speaking the truth. After all, we don't *know.*'

'He wasn't. He was lying. I'm sure of it.'

'Wait until the doctor comes back,' said Tommy. 'Then I'll pass myself off as a journalist anxious to discuss his new system of rest cure with him. That will give me a chance of getting inside and studying the geography of the place.'

The doctor returned about half an hour later. Tommy gave him about five minutes, then he in turn marched up to the front door. But he too returned baffled.

'The doctor was engaged and couldn't be disturbed. And he never sees journalists. Tuppence, you're right. There's something fishy about this place. It's ideally situated—miles from anywhere. Any mortal thing could go on here, and no one would ever know.'

'Come on,' said Tuppence, with determination.

'What are you going to do?'

'I'm going to climb over the wall and see if I can't get up to the house quietly without being seen.'

'Right. I'm with you.'

The garden was somewhat overgrown and afforded a multitude of cover. Tommy and Tuppence managed to reach the back of the house unobserved.

Here there was a wide terrace with some crumbling steps leading down from it. In the middle some french windows opened on to the terrace, but they dared not step out into the open, and the windows where they were crouching were too high for them to be able to look in. It did not seem as though their reconnaissance would be much use, when suddenly Tuppence tightened her grasp of Tommy's arm.

Someone was speaking in the room close to them. The window was open and the fragment of conversation came clearly to their ears.

'Come in, come in, and shut the door,' said a man's

voice irritably. 'A lady came about an hour ago, you said, and asked for Mrs Leigh Gordon?'

Tuppence recognised the answering voice as that of the impassive manservant.

'Yes, sir.'

'You said she wasn't here, of course?'

'Of course, sir.'

'And now this journalist fellow,' fumed the other.

He came suddenly to the window, throwing up the sash, and the two outside, peering through a screen of bushes, recognised Dr Horriston.

'It's the woman I mind most about,' continued the doctor. 'What did she look like?'

'Young, good-looking, and very smartly dressed, sir.'

Tommy nudged Tuppence in the ribs.

'Exactly,' said the doctor between his teeth, 'as I feared. Some friend of the Leigh Gordon woman's. It's getting very difficult. I shall have to take steps—'

He left the sentence unfinished. Tommy and Tuppence heard the door close. There was silence.

Gingerly Tommy led the retreat. When they had reached a little clearing not far away, but out of earshot from the house, he spoke.

'Tuppence, old thing, this is getting serious. They mean mischief. I think we ought to get back to town at once and see Stavansson.'

To his surprise Tuppence shook her head.

'We must stay down here. Didn't you hear him say he was going to take steps—That might mean anything.'

'The worst of it is we've hardly got a case to go to the police on.'

'Listen, Tommy. Why not ring up Stavansson from the village? I'll stay around here.'

'Perhaps that is the best plan,' agreed her husband. 'But I say—Tuppence—'

'Well?'

'Take care of yourself—won't you?'

'Of course I shall, you silly old thing. Cut along.'

It was some two hours later that Tommy returned. He found Tuppence awaiting him near the gate.

'Well?'

'I couldn't get on to Stavansson. Then I tried Lady Susan. She was out too. Then I thought of ringing up old Brady. I asked him to look up Horriston in the Medical Directory or whatever the thing calls itself.'

'Well, what did Dr Brady say?'

'Oh, he knew the name at once. Horriston was once a *bona fide* doctor, but he came a cropper of some kind. Brady called him a most unscrupulous quack, and said he, personally, wouldn't be surprised at anything. The question is, what are we to do now?'

'We must stay here,' said Tuppence instantly. 'I've a feeling they mean something to happen tonight. By the way, a gardener has been clipping ivy round the house. Tommy, *I saw where he put the ladder.*'

'Good for you, Tuppence,' said her husband appreciatively. 'Then tonight—'

'As soon as it's dark—'

'We shall see—'

'What we shall see.'

Tommy took his turn at watching the house whilst Tuppence went to the village and had some food.

Then she returned and they took up the vigil together. At nine o'clock they decided that it was dark enough to commence operations. They were now able to circle round the house in perfect freedom. Suddenly Tuppence clutched Tommy by the arm.

25

'Listen.'

The sound she had heard came again, borne faintly on the night air. It was the moan of a woman in pain. Tuppence pointed upward to a window on the first floor.

'It came from that room,' she whispered.

Again that low moan rent the stillness of the night.

The two listeners decided to put their original plan into action. Tuppence led the way to where she had seen the gardener put the ladder. Between them they carried it to the side of the house from which they had heard the moaning. All the blinds of the ground floor rooms were drawn, but this particular window upstairs was unshuttered.

Tommy put the ladder as noiselessly as possible against the side of the house.

'I'll go up,' whispered Tuppence. 'You stay below. I don't mind climbing ladders and you can steady it better than I could. And in case the doctor should come round the corner you'd be able to deal with him and I shouldn't.'

Nimbly Tuppence swarmed up the ladder and raised her head cautiously to look in at the window. Then she ducked it swiftly, but after a minute or two brought it very slowly up again. She stayed there for about five minutes. Then she descended again.

'It's her,' she said breathlessly and ungrammatically. 'But, oh, Tommy, it's horrible. She's lying there in bed, moaning, and turning to and fro—and just as I got there a woman dressed as a nurse came in. She bent over her and injected something in her arm and then went away again. What shall we do?'

'Is she conscious?'

'I think so. I'm almost sure she is. I fancy she may be

strapped to the bed. I'm going up again, and if I can I'm going to get into that room.'

'I say, Tuppence—'

'If I'm in any sort of danger, I'll yell for you. So long.'

Avoiding further argument Tuppence hurried up the ladder again. Tommy saw her try the window, then noiselessly push up the sash. Another second and she had disappeared inside.

And now an agonising time came for Tommy. He could hear nothing at first. Tuppence and Mrs Leigh Gordon must be talking in whispers if they were talking at all. Presently he did hear a low murmur of voices and drew a breath of relief. But suddenly the voices stopped. Dead silence.

Tommy strained his ears. Nothing. What could they be doing?

Suddenly a hand fell on his shoulder.

'Come on,' said Tuppence's voice out of the darkness.

'Tuppence! How did you get here?'

'Through the front door. Let's get out of this.'

'Get out of this?'

'That's what I said.'

'But—Mrs Leigh Gordon?'

In a tone of indescribable bitterness Tuppence replied: 'Getting thin!'

Tommy looked at her, suspecting irony. 'What do you mean?'

'What I say. Getting thin. Slinkiness. Reduction of weight. Didn't you hear Stavansson say he hated fat women? In the two years he's been away, his Hermy has put on weight. Got a panic when she knew he was coming back and rushed off to do this new treatment of Dr Horriston's. It's injections of some sort, and he makes a deadly secret of it, and charges through the nose.

I dare say he is a quack—but he's a damned successful one! Stavansson comes home a fortnight too soon, when she's only beginning the treatment. Lady Susan has been sworn to secrecy and plays up. And we come down here and make blithering idiots of ourselves!'

Tommy drew a deep breath.

'I believe, Watson,' he said with dignity, 'that there is a very good concert at the Queen's Hall tomorrow. We shall be in plenty of time for it. And you will oblige me by not placing this case upon your records. It has absolutely *no* distinctive features.'

The Herb of Death

'Now then, Mrs B.,' said Sir Henry Clithering encouragingly.

Mrs Bantry, his hostess, looked at him in cold reproof.

'I've told you before that I will *not* be called Mrs B. It's not dignified.'

'Scheherazade, then.'

'And even less am I Sche—what's her name! I never can tell a story properly, ask Arthur if you don't believe me.'

'You're quite good at the facts, Dolly,' said Colonel Bantry, 'but poor at the embroidery.'

'That's just it,' said Mrs Bantry. She flapped the bulb catalogue she was holding on the table in front of her. 'I've been listening to you all and I don't know how you do it. "He said, she said, you wondered, they thought, everyone implied"—well, I just couldn't and there it is! And besides I don't know anything to tell a story about.'

'We can't believe that, Mrs Bantry,' said Dr Lloyd. He shook his grey head in mocking disbelief.

Old Miss Marple said in her gentle voice: 'Surely dear—'

Mrs Bantry continued obstinately to shake her head.

'You don't know how banal my life is. What with the servants and the difficulties of getting scullery maids,

29

and just going to town for clothes, and dentists, and Ascot (which Arthur hates) and then the garden—'

'Ah!' said Dr Lloyd. 'The garden. We all know where your heart lies, Mrs Bantry.'

'It must be nice to have a garden,' said Jane Helier, the beautiful young actress. 'That is, if you hadn't got to dig, or to get your hands messed up. I'm ever so fond of flowers.'

'The garden,' said Sir Henry. 'Can't we take that as a starting point? Come, Mrs B. The poisoned bulb, the deadly daffodils, the herb of death!'

'Now it's odd your saying that,' said Mrs Bantry. 'You've just reminded me. Arthur, do you remember that business at Clodderham Court? You know. Old Sir Ambrose Bercy. Do you remember what a courtly charming old man we thought him?'

'Why, of course. Yes, that *was* a strange business. Go ahead, Dolly.'

'You'd better tell it, dear.'

'Nonsense. Go ahead. Must paddle your own canoe. I did my bit just now.'

Mrs Bantry drew a deep breath. She clasped her hands and her face registered complete mental anguish. She spoke rapidly and fluently.

'Well, there's really not much to tell. The Herb of Death—that's what put it into my head, though in my own mind I call it *sage and onions.*'

'Sage and onions?' asked Dr Lloyd.

Mrs Bantry nodded.

'That was how it happened you see,' she explained. 'We were staying, Arthur and I, with Sir Ambrose Bercy at Clodderham Court, and one day, by mistake (though very stupidly, I've always thought) a lot of foxglove leaves were picked with the sage. The ducks for dinner that night were stuffed with it and everyone was very ill, and one poor girl—Sir Ambrose's ward—died of it.'

She stopped.

'Dear, dear,' said Miss Marple, 'how very tragic.'

'Wasn't it?'

'Well,' said Sir Henry, 'what next?'

'There isn't any next,' said Mrs Bantry, 'that's all.'

Everyone gasped. Though warned beforehand, they had not expected quite such brevity as this.

'But, my dear lady,' remonstrated Sir Henry, 'it can't be all. What you have related is a tragic occurrence, but not in any sense of the word a problem.'

'Well, of course there's some more,' said Mrs Bantry. 'But if I were to tell you it, you'd know what it was.'

She looked defiantly round the assembly and said plaintively:

'I told you I couldn't dress things up and make it sound properly like a story ought to do.'

'Ah ha!' said Sir Henry. He sat up in his chair and adjusted an eyeglass. 'Really, you know, Scheherazade, this is most refreshing. Our ingenuity is challenged. I'm not so sure you haven't done it on purpose—to stimulate our curiosity. A few brisk rounds of "Twenty Questions" is indicated, I think. Miss Marple, will you begin?'

'I'd like to know something about the cook,' said Miss Marple. 'She must have been a very stupid woman, or else very inexperienced.'

'She was just very stupid,' said Mrs Bantry. 'She cried a great deal afterwards and said the leaves had been picked and brought in to her as sage, and how was she to know?'

'Not one who thought for herself,' said Miss Marple.

'Probably an elderly woman and, I dare say, a very good cook?'

'Oh! excellent,' said Mrs Bantry.

'Your turn, Miss Helier,' said Sir Henry.

'Oh! You mean—to ask a question?' There was a pause while Jane pondered. Finally she said helplessly, 'Really—I don't know what to ask.'

Her beautiful eyes looked appealingly at Sir Henry.

'Why not dramatis personae, Miss Helier?' he suggested smiling.

Jane still looked puzzled.

'Characters in order of their appearance,' said Sir Henry gently.

'Oh, yes,' said Jane. 'That's a good idea.'

Mrs Bantry began briskly to tick people off on her fingers.

'Sir Ambrose—Sylvia Keene (that's the girl who died)—a friend of hers who was staying there, Maud Wye, one of those dark ugly girls who manage to make an effort somehow—I never know how they do it. Then there was a Mr Curle who had come down to discuss books with Sir Ambrose—you know, rare books— queer old things in Latin—all musty parchment. There was Jerry Lorimer—he was a kind of next door neighbour. His place, Fairlies, joined Sir Ambrose's estate. And there was Mrs Carpenter, one of those middle-aged pussies who always seem to manage to dig themselves in comfortably somewhere. She was by way of being *dame de compagnie* to Sylvia, I suppose.'

'If it is my turn,' said Sir Henry, 'and I suppose it is, as I'm sitting next to Miss Helier, I want a good deal. I want a short verbal portrait, please, Mrs Bantry, of all the foregoing.'

'Oh!' Mrs Bantry hesitated.

'Sir Ambrose now,' continued Sir Henry. 'Start with him. What was he like?'

'Oh! he was a very distinguished-looking old man—and not so very old really—not more than sixty, I suppose. But he was very delicate—he had a weak heart, could never go upstairs—he had to have a lift put in, and so that made him seem older than he was. Very charming manners—*courtly*—that's the word that describes him best. You never saw him ruffled or upset. He had beautiful white hair and a particularly charming voice.'

'Good,' said Sir Henry. 'I see Sir Ambrose. Now the girl Sylvia—what did you say her name was?'

'Sylvia Keene. She was pretty—really *very* pretty. Fair-haired, you know, and a lovely skin. Not, perhaps, very clever. In fact, rather stupid.'

'Oh! come, Dolly,' protested her husband.

'Arthur, of course, wouldn't think so,' said Mrs Bantry drily. 'But she *was* stupid—she really never said anything worth listening to.'

'One of the most graceful creatures I ever saw,' said Colonel Bantry warmly. 'See her playing tennis—charming, simply charming. And she was full of fun—most amusing little thing. And such a pretty way with her. I bet the young fellows all thought so.'

'That's just where you're wrong,' said Mrs Bantry. 'Youth, as such, has no charms for young men nowadays. It's only old buffers like you, Arthur, who sit maundering on about young girls.'

'Being young's no good,' said Jane. 'You've got to have SA.'

'What,' said Miss Marple, 'is SA?'

'Sex appeal,' said Jane.

'Ah! yes,' said Miss Marple. 'What in my day they used to call "having the come hither in your eye".'

'Not a bad description,' said Sir Henry. 'The *dame de*

33

compagnie you described, I think, as a pussy, Mrs Bantry?'

'I didn't mean a *cat*, you know,' said Mrs Bantry. 'It's quite different. Just a big soft white purry person. Always very sweet. That's what Adelaide Carpenter was like.'

'What sort of aged woman?'

'Oh! I should say fortyish. She'd been there some time—ever since Sylvia was eleven, I believe. A very tactful person. One of those widows left in unfortunate circumstances with plenty of aristocratic relations, but no ready cash. I didn't like her myself—but then I never do like people with very white long hands. And I don't like pussies.'

'Mr Curle?'

'Oh! one of those elderly stooping men. There are so many of them about, you'd hardly know one from the other. He showed enthusiasm when talking about his musty books, but not at any other time. I don't think Sir Ambrose knew him very well.'

'And Jerry next door?'

'A really charming boy. He was engaged to Sylvia. That's what made it so sad.'

'Now I wonder—' began Miss Marple, and then stopped. 'What?'

'Nothing, dear.'

Sir Henry looked at the old lady curiously. Then he said thoughtfully:

'So this young couple were engaged. Had they been engaged long?'

'About a year. Sir Ambrose had opposed the engagement on the plea that Sylvia was too young. But after a year's engagement he had given in and the marriage was to have taken place quite soon.'

'Ah! Had the young lady any property?'

34

'Next to nothing—a bare hundred or two a year.'

'No rat in that hole, Clithering,' said Colonel Bantry, and laughed.

'It's the doctor's turn to ask a question,' said Sir Henry. 'I stand down.'

'My curiosity is mainly professional,' said Dr Lloyd. 'I should like to know what medical evidence was given at the inquest—that is, if our hostess remembers, or, indeed, if she knows.'

'I know roughly,' said Mrs Bantry. 'It was poisoning by digitalin—is that right?'

Dr Lloyd nodded.

'The active principle of the foxglove—digitalis—acts on the heart. Indeed, it is a very valuable drug in some forms of heart trouble. A very curious case altogther. I would never have believed that eating a preparation of foxglove leaves could possibly result fatally. These ideas of eating poisonous leaves and berries are very much exaggerated. Very few people realize that the vital principle, or alkaloid, has to be extracted with much care and preparation.'

'Mrs MacArthur sent some special bulbs round to Mrs Toomie the other day,' said Miss Marple. 'And Mrs Toomie's cook mistook them for onions, and all the Toomies were very ill indeed.'

'But they didn't die of it,' said Dr Lloyd.

'No. They didn't die of it,' admitted Miss Marple.

'A girl I knew died of ptomaine poisoning,' said Jane Helier.

'We must get on with investigating the crime,' said Sir Henry.

'Crime?' said Jane, startled. 'I thought it was an accident.'

'If it were an accident,' said Sir Henry gently, 'I do not

think Mrs Bantry would have told us this story. No, as I read it, this was an accident only in appearance—behind it is something more sinister. I remember a case—various guests in a house party were chatting after dinner. The walls were adorned with all kinds of old-fashioned weapons. Entirely as a joke one of the party seized an ancient horse pistol and pointed it at another man, pretending to fire it. The pistol was loaded and went off, killing the man. We had to ascertain in that case, first, who had secretly prepared and loaded that pistol, and secondly who had so led and directed the conversation that that final bit of horseplay resulted—for the man who had fired the pistol was entirely innocent!

'It seems to me we have much the same problem here. Those digitalin leaves were deliberately mixed with the sage, knowing what the result would be. Since we exonerate the cook—we do exonerate the cook, don't we?—the question arises: Who picked the leaves and delivered them to the kitchen?'

'That's easily answered,' said Mrs Bantry. 'At least the last part of it is. It was Sylvia herself who took the leaves to the kitchen. It was part of her daily job to gather things like salad or herbs, bunches of young carrots—all the sort of things that gardeners never pick right. They hate giving you anything young and tender—they wait for them to be fine specimens. Sylvia and Mrs Carpenter used to see to a lot of these things themselves. And there was foxglove actually growing all amongst the sage in one corner, so the mistake was quite natural.'

'But did Sylvia actually pick them herself?'

'That, nobody ever knew. It was assumed so.'

'Assumptions,' said Sir Henry, 'are dangerous things.'

'But I do know that Mrs Carpenter didn't pick them,' said Mrs Bantry. 'Because, as it happened, she was walking with me on the terrace that morning. We went out there after breakfast. It was unusually nice and warm for early spring. Sylvia went alone down into the garden, but later I saw her walking arm-in-arm with Maud Wye.'

'So they were great friends, were they?' asked Miss Marple.

'Yes,' said Mrs Bantry. She seemed as though about to say something, but did not do so.

'Had she been staying there long?' asked Miss Marple.

'About a fortnight,' said Mrs Bantry.

There was a note of trouble in her voice.

'You didn't like Miss Wye?' suggested Sir Henry.

'I did. That's just it. I did.'

The trouble in her voice had grown to distress.

'You're keeping something back, Mrs Bantry,' said Sir Henry accusingly.

'I wondered just now,' said Miss Marple, 'but I didn't like to go on.'

'When did you wonder?'

'When you said that the young people were engaged. You said that that was what made it so sad. But, if you know what I mean, your voice didn't sound right when you said it—not convincing, you know.'

'What a dreadful person you are,' said Mrs Bantry. 'You always seem to *know*. Yes, I was thinking of something. But I don't really know whether I ought to say it or not.'

'You must say it,' said Sir Henry. 'Whatever your scruples, it mustn't be kept back.'

'Well, it was just this,' said Mrs Bantry. 'One evening—in fact the very evening before the tragedy—I happened to go out on the terrace before dinner. The window in the drawing-room was open. And as it

chanced I saw Jerry Lorimer and Maud Wye. He was—
well—kissing her. Of course I didn't know whether
it was just a sort of chance affair, or whether—well, I
mean, one can't *tell*. I knew Sir Ambrose never had
really liked Jerry Lorimer—so perhaps he knew he was
that kind of young man. But one thing I *am* sure of:
that girl, Maud Wye, was *really* fond of him. You'd only
to see her looking at him when she was off guard. And
I think, too, they were really better suited than he and
Sylvia were.'

'I am going to ask a question quickly, before Miss
Marple can,' said Sir Henry. 'I want to know whether,
after the tragedy, Jerry Lorimer married Maud Wye?'

'Yes,' said Mrs Bantry. 'He did. Six months afterwards.'

'Oh! Scheherezade, Scheherezade,' said Sir Henry.
'To think of the way you told us this story at first! Bare
bones indeed—and to think of the amount of flesh
we're finding on them now.'

'Don't speak so ghoulishly,' said Mrs Bantry. 'And
don't use the word flesh. Vegetarians always do. They
say, "I never eat flesh" in a way that puts you right off
your little beefsteak. Mr Curle was a vegetarian. He
used to eat some peculiar stuff that looked like bran for
breakfast. Those elderly stooping men with beards are
often faddy. They have patent kinds of underwear, too.'

'What on earth, Dolly,' said her husband, 'do you
know about Mr Curle's underwear?'

'Nothing,' said Mrs Bantry with dignity. 'I was just
making a guess.'

'I'll amend my former statement,' said Sir Henry. 'I'll
say instead that the dramatis personae in your problem
are very interesting. I'm beginning to see them all—eh,
Miss Marple?'

'Human nature is always interesting, Sir Henry. And it's curious to see how certain types always tend to act in exactly the same way.'

'Two women and a man,' said Sir Henry. 'The old eternal human triangle. Is that the base of our problem here? I rather fancy it is.'

Dr Lloyd cleared his throat.

'I've been thinking,' he said rather diffidently. 'Do you say, Mrs Bantry, that you yourself were ill?'

'Was I not! So was Arthur! So was everyone!'

'That's just it—everyone,' said the doctor. 'You see what I mean? In Sir Henry's story which he told us just now, one man shot another—he didn't have to shoot the whole room full.'

'I don't understand,' said Jane. 'Who shot who?'

'I'm saying that whoever planned this thing went about it very curiously, either with a blind belief in chance, or else with an absolutely reckless disregard for human life. I can hardly believe there is a man capable of deliberately poisoning eight people with the object of removing one amongst them.'

'I see your point,' said Sir Henry, thoughtfully. 'I confess I ought to have thought of that.'

'And mightn't he have poisoned himself too?' asked Jane.

'Was anyone absent from dinner that night?' asked Miss Marple. Mrs Bantry shook her head.

'Everyone was there.'

'Except Mr Lorimer, I suppose, my dear. He wasn't staying in the house, was he?'

'No; but he was dining there that evening,' said Mrs Bantry.

'Oh!' said Miss Marple in a changed voice. 'That makes all the difference in the world.'

She frowned vexedly to herself.

'I've been very stupid,' she murmured. 'Very stupid indeed.'

'I confess your point worries me, Lloyd,' said Sir Henry.

'How ensure that the girl, and the girl only, should get a fatal dose?'

'You can't,' said the doctor. 'That brings me to the point I'm going to make. *Supposing the girl was not the intended victim after all?*'

'What?'

'In all cases of food poisoning, the result is very uncertain. Several people share a dish. What happens? One or two are slightly ill, two more, say, are seriously indisposed, one dies. That's the way of it—there's no certainty anywhere. But there are cases where another factor might enter in. Digitalin is a drug that acts directly on the heart—as I've told you it's prescribed in certain cases. *Now, there was one person in that house who suffered from a heart complaint.* Suppose he was the victim selected? What would not be fatal to the rest *would* be fatal to him—or so the murderer might reasonably suppose. That the thing turned out differently is only a proof of what I was saying just now—the uncertainty and unreliability of the effects of drugs on human beings.'

'Sir Ambrose,' said Sir Henry, 'you think *he* was the person aimed at? Yes, yes—and the girl's death was a mistake.'

'Who got his money after he was dead?' asked Jane.

'A very sound question, Miss Helier. One of the first we always ask in my late profession,' said Sir Henry.

'Sir Ambrose had a son,' said Mrs Bantry slowly. 'He had quarrelled with him many years previously. The boy was wild, I believe. Still, it was not in Sir Ambrose's power to disinherit him—Clodderham Court was entailed. Martin Bercy succeeded to the title and estate. There was, however, a good deal of other property that Sir Ambrose could leave as he chose, and that he left to his ward Sylvia. I know this because Sir Ambrose died less than a year after the events I am telling you of, and he had not troubled to make a new will after Sylvia's death. I think the money went to the Crown—or perhaps it was to his son as next of kin—I don't really remember.'

'So it was only to the interest of a son who wasn't there and the girl who died herself to make away with him,' said Sir Henry thoughtfully. 'That doesn't seem very promising.'

'Didn't the other woman get anything?' asked Jane. 'The one Mrs Bantry calls the Pussy woman.'

'She wasn't mentioned in the will,' said Mrs Bantry.

'Miss Marple, you're not listening,' said Sir Henry. 'You're somewhere far away.'

'I was thinking of old Mr Badger, the chemist,' said Miss Marple. 'He had a very young housekeeper—young enough to be not only his daughter, but his grand-daughter. Not a word to anyone, and his family, a lot of nephews and nieces, full of expectations. And when he died, would you believe it, he'd been secretly married to her for two years? Of course Mr Badger was a chemist, and a very rude, common old man as well, and Sir Ambrose Bercy was a very courtly gentleman, so Mrs Bantry says, but for all that human nature is much the same everywhere.'

There was a pause. Sir Henry looked very hard at Miss Marple who looked back at him with gently quizzical blue eyes. Jane Helier broke the silence.

'Was this Mrs Carpenter good-looking?' she asked.

'Yes, in a very quiet way. Nothing startling.'

'She had a very sympathetic voice,' said Colonel Bantry.

'Purring—that's what I call it,' said Mrs Bantry. 'Purring!'

'You'll be called a cat yourself one of these days, Dolly.'

'I like being a cat in my home circle,' said Mrs Bantry. 'I don't much like women anyway, and you know it. I like men and flowers.'

'Excellent taste,' said Sir Henry. 'Especially in putting men first.'

'That was tact,' said Mrs Bantry. 'Well, now, what about my little problem? I've been quite fair, I think. Arthur, don't you think I've been fair?'

'Yes, my dear. I don't think there'll be any inquiry into the running by the stewards of the Jockey Club.'

'First boy,' said Mrs Bantry, pointing a finger at Sir Henry.

'I'm going to be long-winded. Because, you see, I haven't really got any feeling of certainty about the matter. First, Sir Ambrose. Well, he wouldn't take such an original method of committing suicide—and on the other hand he certainly had nothing to gain by the death of his ward. Exit Sir Ambrose. Mr Curle. No motive for death of girl. If Sir Ambrose was intended victim, he might possibly have purloined a rare manuscript or two that no one else would miss. Very thin and most unlikely. So I think, that in spite of Mrs Bantry's suspicions as to his underclothing, Mr Curle is cleared. Miss Wye. Motive for death of Sir Ambrose—none. Motive for death of Sylvia pretty strong. She wanted Sylvia's young man, and wanted him rather badly—from Mrs Bantry's account. She was with Sylvia that morning in the garden, so had opportunity to pick leaves. No, we can't dismiss

Miss Wye so easily. Young Lorimer. He's got a motive in either case. If he gets rid of his sweetheart, he can marry the other girl. Still it seems a bit drastic to kill her—what's a broken engagement these days? If Sir Ambrose dies, he will marry a rich girl instead of a poor one. That might be important or not—depends on his financial position. If I find that his estate was heavily mortgaged and that Mrs Bantry has deliberately withheld that fact from us, I shall claim a foul. Now Mrs Carpenter. You know, I have suspicions of Mrs Carpenter. Those white hands, for one thing, and her excellent alibi at the time the herbs were picked—I always distrust alibis. And I've got another reason for suspecting her which I will keep to myself. Still, on the whole, if I've got to plump, I shall plump for Miss Maude Wye, because there's more evidence against her than anyone else.'

'Next boy,' said Mrs Bantry, and pointed at Dr Lloyd.

'I think you're wrong, Clithering, in sticking to the theory that the girl's death was meant. I am convinced that the murderer intended to do away with Sir Ambrose. I don't think that young Lorimer had the necessary knowledge. I am inclined to believe that Mrs Carpenter was the guilty party. She had been a long time with the family, knew all about the state of Sir Ambrose's health, and could easily arrange for this girl Sylvia (who, you said yourself, was rather stupid) to pick the right leaves. Motive, I confess, I don't see; but I hazard the guess that Sir Ambrose had at one time made a will in which she was mentioned. That's the best I can do.'

Mrs Bantry's pointing finger went on to Jane Helier.

'I don't know what to say,' said Jane, 'except this: Why shouldn't the girl herself have done it? She took the leaves into the kitchen after all. And you say Sir Ambrose had been sticking out against her marriage.

43

If he died, she'd get the money and be able to marry at once. She'd know just as much about Sir Ambrose's health as Mrs Carpenter would.'

Mrs Bantry's finger came slowly round to Miss Marple.

'Now then, School Marm,' she said.

'Sir Henry has put it all very clearly—very clearly indeed,' said Miss Marple. 'And Dr Lloyd was so right in what he said. Between them they seem to have made things so very clear. Only I don't think Dr Lloyd quite realized one aspect of what he said. You see, not being Sir Ambrose's medical adviser, he couldn't know just what kind of heart trouble Sir Ambrose had, could he?'

'I don't quite see what you mean, Miss Marple,' said Dr Lloyd.

'You're assuming—aren't you?—that Sir Ambrose had the kind of heart that digitalin would affect adversely? But there's nothing to prove that that's so. It might be just the other way about.'

'The other way about?'

'Yes, you did say that it was often prescribed for heart trouble?'

'Even then, Miss Marple, I don't see what that leads to?'

'Well, it would mean that he would have digitalin in his possession quite naturally—without having to account for it. What I am trying to say (I always express myself so badly) is this: Supposing you wanted to poison anyone with a fatal dose of digitalin. Wouldn't the simplest and easiest way be to arrange for everyone to be poisoned—actually by digitalin leaves? It wouldn't be fatal in anyone else's case, of course, but no one would be surprised at one victim because, as Dr Lloyd said, these things are so uncertain. No one would be

44

likely to ask whether the girl had actually had a fatal dose of infusion of digitalis or something of that kind. He might have put it in a cocktail, or in her coffee or even made her drink it quite simply as a tonic.'

'You mean Sir Ambrose poisoned his ward, the charming girl whom he loved?'

'That's just it,' said Miss Marple. 'Like Mr Badger and his young housekeeper. Don't tell me it's absurd for a man of sixty to fall in love with a girl of twenty. It happens every day—and I dare say with an old autocrat like Sir Ambrose, it might take him queerly. These things become a madness sometimes. He couldn't bear the thought of her getting married—did his best to oppose it—and failed. His mad jealousy became so great that he preferred killing her to letting her go to young Lorimer. He must have thought of it some time beforehand, because that foxglove seed would have to be sown among the sage. He'd pick it himself when the time came, and send her into the kitchen with it. It's horrible to think of, but I suppose we must take as merciful a view of it as we can. Gentlemen of that age are sometimes very peculiar indeed where young girls are concerned. Our last organist—but there, I mustn't talk scandal.'

'Mrs Bantry,' said Sir Henry. 'Is this so?'

Mrs Bantry nodded.

'Yes. I'd no idea of it—never dreamed of the thing being anything but an accident. Then, after Sir Ambrose's death, I got a letter. He had left directions to send it to me. He told me the truth in it. I don't know why—but he and I always got on very well together.'

In the momentary silence, she seemed to feel an unspoken criticism and went on hastily:

'You think I'm betraying a confidence—but that isn't

so. I've changed all the names. He wasn't really called Sir Ambrose Bercy. Didn't you see how Arthur stared stupidly when I said that name to him? He didn't understand at first. I've changed everything. It's like they say in magazines and in the beginning of books: "All the characters in this story are purely fictitious." You never know who they really are.'

How Does Your Garden Grow?

Hercule Poirot arranged his letters in a neat pile in front of him. He picked up the topmost letter, studied the address for a moment, then neatly slit the back of the envelope with a little paper-knife that he kept on the breakfast table for that express purpose and extracted the contents. Inside was yet another envelope, carefully sealed with purple wax and marked 'Private and Confidential'.

Hercule Poirot's eyebrows rose a little on his egg-shaped head. He murmured, '*Patience! Nous allons arriver!*' and once more brought the little paper-knife into play. This time the envelope yielded a letter—written in a rather shaky and spiky handwriting. Several words were heavily underlined.

Hercule Poirot unfolded it and read. The letter was headed once again 'Private and Confidential'. On the right-hand side was the address—Rosebank, Charman's Green, Bucks—and the date—March twenty-first.

Dear M. Poirot,

I have been recommended to you by an old and valued friend of mine who knows the *worry* and *distress* I have been in lately.

Not that this friend knows the actual *circumstances*—those I have kept *entirely* to myself—the matter being

47

strictly private. My friend assures me that you are *discretion* itself—and that there will be no fear of my being involved in a *police* matter which, if my suspicions should prove correct, I should *very much dislike*. But it is of course possible that I am *entirely* mistaken. I do not feel myself clear-headed enough nowadays—suffering as I do from insomnia and the result of a severe illness last winter—to investigate things for myself. I have neither the *means* nor the *ability*. On the other hand, I must reiterate once more that this is a very delicate family matter and that for many reasons I may want the *whole thing hushed up*.

If I am once assured of the *facts*, I can deal with the matter myself and should prefer to do so. I hope that I have made myself clear on this point. If you will undertake this investigation perhaps you will let me know to the above address?

Yours very truly,

AMELIA BARROWBY

Poirot read the letter through twice. Again his eyebrows rose slightly. Then he placed it on one side and proceeded to the next envelope in the pile.

At ten o'clock precisely he entered the room where Miss Lemon, his confidential secretary, sat awaiting her instructions for the day. Miss Lemon was forty-eight and of unprepossessing appearance. Her general effect was that of a lot of bones flung together at random. She had a passion for order almost equalling that of Poirot himself; and though capable of thinking, she never thought unless told to do so.

Poirot handed her the morning correspondence. 'Have the goodness, mademoiselle, to write refusals couched in correct terms to all of these.'

Miss Lemon ran an eye over the various letters, scribbling in turn a hieroglyphic on each of them. These marks were legible to her alone and were in a code of her own: 'Soft soap'; 'slap in the face'; 'purr purr'; 'curt'; and so on. Having done this, she nodded and looked up for further instructions.

Poirot handed her Amelia Barrowby's letter. She extracted it from its double envelope, read it through and looked up inquiringly.

'Yes, M. Poirot?' Her pencil hovered—ready—over her shorthand pad.

'What is your opinion of that letter, Miss Lemon?'

With a slight frown Miss Lemon put down the pencil and read through the letter again.

The contents of a letter meant nothing to Miss Lemon except from the point of view of composing an adequate reply. Very occasionally her employer appealed to her human, as opposed to her official, capacities. It slightly annoyed Miss Lemon when he did so—she was very nearly the perfect machine, completely and gloriously uninterested in all human affairs. Her real passion in life was the perfection of a filing system beside which all other filing systems should sink into oblivion. She dreamed of such a system at night. Nevertheless, Miss Lemon was perfectly capable of intelligence on purely human matters, as Hercule Poirot well knew.

'Well?' he demanded.

'Old lady,' said Miss Lemon. 'Got the wind up pretty badly.'

'Ah! The wind rises in her, you think?'

Miss Lemon, who considered that Poirot had been long enough in Great Britain to understand its slang terms, did not reply. She took a brief look at the double envelope.

'Very hush-hush,' she said. 'And tells you nothing at all.'

'Yes,' said Hercule Poirot. 'I observed that.'

Miss Lemon's hand hung once more hopefully over the shorthand pad. This time Hercule Poirot responded.

'Tell her I will do myself the honour to call upon her at any time she suggests, unless she prefers to consult me here. Do not type the letter—write it by hand.'

'Yes, M. Poirot.'

Poirot produced more correspondence. 'These are bills.'

Miss Lemon's efficient hands sorted them quickly. 'I'll pay all but these two.'

'Why those two? There is no error in them.'

'They are firms you've only just begun to deal with. It looks bad to pay too promptly when you've just opened an account—looks as though you were working up to get some credit later on.'

'Ah!' murmured Poirot. 'I bow to your superior knowledge of the British tradesman.'

'There's nothing much I don't know about them,' said Miss Lemon grimly.

The letter to Miss Amelia Barrowby was duly written and sent, but no reply was forthcoming. Perhaps, thought Hercule Poirot, the old lady had unravelled her mystery herself. Yet he felt a shade of surprise that in that case she should not have written a courteous word to say that his services were no longer required.

It was five days later when Miss Lemon, after receiving her morning's instructions, said, 'That Miss Barrowby we wrote to—no wonder there's been no answer. She's dead.'

Hercule Poirot said very softly, 'Ah—dead.' It sounded not so much like a question as an answer.

Opening her handbag, Miss Lemon produced a newspaper cutting. 'I saw it in the tube and tore it out.'

Just registering in his mind approval of the fact that, though Miss Lemon used the word 'tore', she had neatly cut the entry with scissors, Poirot read the announcement taken from the Births, Deaths and Marriages in the *Morning Post*: 'On March 26th—suddenly—at Rosebank, Charman's Green, Amelia Jan Barrowby, in her seventy-third year. No flowers, by request.'

Poirot read it over. He murmured under his breath, 'Suddenly.' Then he said briskly, 'If you will be so obliging as to take a letter, Miss Lemon?'

The pencil hovered. Miss Lemon, her mind dwelling on the intricacies of the filing system, took down in rapid and correct shorthand:

Dear Miss Barrowby,

I have received no reply from you, but as I shall be in the neighbourhood of Charman's Green on Friday, I will call upon you on that day and discuss more fully the matter mentioned to me in your letter.

Yours, etc.

'Type this letter, please; and if it is posted at once, it should get to Charman's Green tonight.'

On the following morning a letter in a black-edged envelope arrived by the second post:

Dear Sir,

In reply to your letter my aunt, Miss Barrowby, passed away on the twenty-sixth, so the matter you speak of is no longer of importance.

Yours truly,

MARY DELAFONTAINE

Poirot smiled to himself. 'No longer of importance . . . Ah—that is what we shall see. *En avant*—to Charman's Green.'

Rosebank was a house that seemed likely to live up to its name, which is more than can be said for most houses of its class and character.

Hercule Poirot paused as he walked up the path to the front door and looked approvingly at the neatly planned beds on either side of him. Rose trees that promised a good harvest later in the year, and at present daffodils, early tulips, blue hyacinths—the last bed was partly edged with shells.

Poirot murmured to himself, 'How does it go, the English rhyme the children sing?

> 'Mistress Mary, quite contrary,
> How does your garden grow?
> With cockle-shells, and silver bells,
> And pretty maids all in a row.

'Not a row, perhaps,' he considered, 'but here is at least one pretty maid to make the little rhyme come right.'

The front door had opened and a neat little maid in cap and apron was looking somewhat dubiously at the spectacle of a heavily moustached foreign gentleman talking aloud to himself in the front garden. She was, as Poirot had noted, a very pretty little maid, with round blue eyes and rosy cheeks.

Poirot raised his hat with courtesy and addressed her: 'Pardon, but does a Miss Amelia Barrowby live here?'

The little maid gasped and her eyes grew rounder. 'Oh, sir, didn't you know? She's dead. Ever so sudden it was. Tuesday night.'

She hesitated, divided between two strong instincts: the first, distrust of a foreigner; the second, the pleasurable enjoyment of her class in dwelling on the subject of illness and death.

'You amaze me,' said Hercule Poirot, not very truthfully. 'I had an appointment with the lady for today. However, I can perhaps see the other lady who lives here.'

The little maid seemed slightly doubtful. 'The mistress? Well, you could see her, perhaps, but I don't know whether she'll be seeing anyone or not.'

'She will see me,' said Poirot, and handed her a card.

The authority of his tone had its effect. The rosy-cheeked maid fell back and ushered Poirot into a sitting-room on the right of the hall. Then, card in hand, she departed to summon her mistress.

Hercule Poirot looked round him. The room was a perfectly conventional drawing-room—oatmeal-coloured paper with a frieze round the top, indeterminate cretonnes, rose-coloured cushions and curtains, a good many china knick-knacks and ornaments. There was nothing in the room that stood out, that announced a definite personality.

Suddenly Poirot, who was very sensitive, felt eyes watching him. He wheeled round. A girl was standing in the entrance of the french window—a small, sallow girl, with very black hair and suspicious eyes.

She came in, and as Poirot made a little bow she burst out abruptly, 'Why have you come?'

Poirot did not reply. He merely raised his eyebrows.

'You are not a lawyer—no?' Her English was good, but not for a minute would anyone have taken her to be English.

'Why should I be a lawyer, mademoiselle?'

The girl stared at him sullenly. 'I thought you might be. I thought you had come perhaps to say that she did not know what she was doing. I have heard of such things—the not due influence; that is what they call it, no? But that is not right. She wanted me to have the money, and I shall have it. If it is needful I shall have a lawyer of my own. The money is mine. She wrote it down so, and so it shall be.' She looked ugly, her chin thrust out, her eyes gleaming.

The door opened and a tall woman entered and said, 'Katrina.'

The girl shrank, flushed, muttered something and went out through the window.

Poirot turned to face the newcomer who had so effectually dealt with the situation by uttering a single word. There had been authority in her voice, and contempt and a shade of well-bred irony. He realized at once that this was the owner of the house, Mary Delafontaine.

'M. Poirot? I wrote to you. You cannot have received my letter.'

'Alas, I have been away from London.'

'Oh, I see; that explains it. I must introduce myself. My name is Delafontaine. This is my husband. Miss Barrowby was my aunt.'

Mr Delafontaine had entered so quietly that his arrival had passed unnoticed. He was a tall man with grizzled hair and an indeterminate manner. He had a nervous way of fingering his chin. He looked often towards his wife, and it was plain that he expected her to take the lead in any conversation.

'I must regret that I intrude in the midst of your bereavement,' said Hercule Poirot.

'I quite realize that it is not your fault,' said Mrs

Delafontaine. 'My aunt died on Tuesday evening. It was quite unexpected.'

'Most unexpected,' said Mr Delafontaine. 'Great blow.' His eyes watched the window where the foreign girl had disappeared.

'I apologize,' said Hercule Poirot. 'And I withdraw.' He moved a step towards the door.

'Half a sec,' said Mr Delafontaine. 'You—er—had an appointment with Aunt Amelia, you say?'

'*Parfaitement.*'

'Perhaps you will tell us about it,' said his wife. 'If there is anything we can do—'

'It was of a private nature,' said Poirot. 'I am a detective,' he added simply.

Mr Delafontaine knocked over a little china figure he was handling. His wife looked puzzled.

'A detective? And you had an appointment with Auntie? But how extraordinary!' She stared at him. 'Can't you tell us a little more, M. Poirot? It—it seems quite fantastic.'

Poirot was silent for a moment. He chose his words with care.

'It is difficult for me, madame, to know what to do.'

'Look here,' said Mr Delafontaine. 'She didn't mention Russians, did she?'

'Russians?'

'Yes, you know—Bolshies, Reds, all that sort of thing.'

'Don't be absurd, Henry,' said his wife.

Mr Delafontaine collapsed. 'Sorry—sorry—I just wondered.'

Mary Delafontaine looked frankly at Poirot. Her eyes were very blue—the colour of forget-me-nots. 'If you can tell us anything, M. Poirot, I should be glad if you would do so. I can assure you that I have a—a reason for asking.'

Mr Delafontaine looked alarmed. 'Be careful, old girl—you know there may be nothing in it.'

Again his wife quelled him with a glance. 'Well, M. Poirot?'

Slowly, gravely, Hercule Poirot shook his head. He shook it with visible regret, but he shook it. 'At present, madame,' he said, 'I fear I must say nothing.'

He bowed, picked up his hat and moved to the door. Mary Delafontaine came with him into the hall. On the doorstep he paused and looked at her.

'You are fond of your garden, I think, madame?'

'I? Yes, I spend a lot of time gardening.'

Je vous fais mes compliments.

He bowed once more and strode down to the gate. As he passed out of it and turned to the right he glanced back and registered two impressions—a sallow face watching him from the first-floor window, and a man of erect and soldierly carriage pacing up and down on the opposite side of the street.

Hercule Poirot nodded to himself. *'Definitivement,'* he said. 'There is a mouse in this hole! What move must the cat make now?'

His decision took him to the nearest post office. Here he put through a couple of telephone calls. The result seemed to be satisfactory. He bent his steps to Charman's Green police station, where he inquired for Inspector Sims.

Inspector Sims was a big, burly man with a hearty manner. 'M. Poirot?' he inquired. 'I thought so. I've just this minute had a telephone call through from the chief constable about you. He said you'd be dropping in. Come into my office.'

The door shut, the inspector waved Poirot to one chair, settled himself in another, and turned a gaze of acute inquiry upon his visitor.

'You're very quick on to the mark, M. Poirot. Come to see us about this Rosebank case almost before we know it is a case. What put you on to it?'

Poirot drew out the letter he had received and handed it to the inspector. The latter read it with some interest.

'Interesting,' he said. 'The trouble is, it might mean so many things. Pity she couldn't have been a little more explicit. It would have helped us now.'

'Or there might have been no need for help.'

'You mean?'

'She might have been alive.'

'You go as far as that, do you? H'm—I'm not sure you're wrong.'

'I pray of you, Inspector, recount to me the facts. I know nothing at all.'

'That's easily done. Old lady was taken bad after dinner on Tuesday night. Very alarming. Convulsions—spasms—whatnot. They sent for the doctor. By the time he arrived she was dead. Idea was she'd died of a fit. Well, he didn't much like the look of things. He hemmed and hawed and put it with a bit of soft sawder, but he made it clear that he couldn't give a death certificate. And as far as the family go, that's where the matter stands. They're awaiting the result of the post-mortem. We've got a bit further. The doctor gave us the tip right away—he and the police surgeon did the autopsy together—and the result is in no doubt whatever. The old lady died of a large dose of strychnine.'

'Aha!'

'That's right. Very nasty bit of work. Point is, who

57

gave it to her? It must have been administered very shortly before death. First idea was it was given to her in her food at dinner—but, frankly, that seems to be a washout. They had artichoke soup, served from a tureen, fish pie and apple tart.

'Miss Barrowby, Mr Delafontaine and Mrs Delafontaine. Miss Barrowby had a kind of nurse-attendant—a half-Russian girl—but she didn't eat with the family. She had the remains as they came out from the dining-room. There's a maid, but it was her night out. She left the soup on the stove and the fish pie in the oven, and the apple tart was cold. All three of them ate the same thing—and, apart from that, I don't think you could get strychnine down anyone's throat that way. Stuff's as bitter as gall. The doctor told me you could taste it in a solution of one in a thousand, or something like that.'

'Coffee?'

'Coffee's more like it, but the old lady never took coffee.'

'I see your point. Yes, it seems an insuperable difficulty. What did she drink at the meal?'

'Water.'

'Worse and worse.'

'Bit of a teaser, isn't it?'

'She had money, the old lady?'

'Very well to do, I imagine. Of course, we haven't got exact details yet. The Delafontaines are pretty badly off, from what I can make out. The old lady helped with the upkeep of the house.'

Poirot smiled a little. He said, 'So you suspect the Delafontaines. Which of them?'

'I don't exactly say I suspect either of them in particular. But there it is; they're her only near relations, and her death brings them a tidy sum of money, I've no doubt. We all know what human nature is!'

'Sometimes inhuman—yes, that is very true. And there was nothing else the old lady ate or drank?'

'Well, as a matter of fact—'

'Ah, *voilà*! I felt that you had something, as you say, up your sleeve—the soup, the fish pie, the apple tart—a *bêtise*! Now we come to the hub of the affair.'

'I don't know about that. But as a matter of fact, the old girl took a cachet before meals. You know, not a pill or a tablet; one of those rice-paper things with a powder inside. Some perfectly harmless thing for the digestion.'

'Admirable. Nothing is easier than to fill a cachet with strychnine and substitute it for one of the others. It slips down the throat with a drink of water and is not tasted.'

'That's all right. The trouble is, the girl gave it to her.'

'The Russian girl?'

'Yes. Katrina Rieger. She was a kind of lady-help, nurse-companion to Miss Barrowby. Fairly ordered about by her, too, I gather. Fetch this, fetch that, fetch the other, rub my back, pour out my medicine, run round to the chemist—all that sort of business. You know how it is with these old women—they mean to be kind, but what they need is a sort of black slave!'

Poirot smiled.

'And there you are, you see,' continued Inspector Sims. 'It doesn't fit in what you might call nicely. Why should the girl poison her? Miss Barrowby dies and now the girl will be out of a job, and jobs aren't easy to find—she's not trained or anything.'

'Still,' suggested Poirot, 'if the box of cachets was left about, anyone in the house might have the opportunity.'

'Naturally we're making inquiries—quiet like, if you understand me. When the prescription was last made up, where it was usually kept; patience and a lot of spade work—that's what will do the trick in the end. And then there's Miss Barrowby's solicitor. I'm having an interview with him tomorrow. And the bank manager. There's a lot to be done still.'

Poirot rose. 'A little favour, Inspector Sims; you will send me a little word how the affair marches. I would esteem it a great favour. Here is my telephone number.'

'Why, certainly, M. Poirot. Two heads are better than one; and besides, you ought to be in on this, having had that letter and all.'

'You are too amiable, Inspector.' Politely, Poirot shook hands and took his leave.

He was called to the telephone on the following afternoon. 'Is that M. Poirot? Inspector Sims here. Things are beginning to sit up and look pretty in the little matter you and I know of.'

'In verity? Tell me, I pray of you.'

'Well, here's item No. I—and a pretty big item. Miss B. left a small legacy to her niece and everything else to K. In consideration of her great kindness and attention—that's the way it was put. That alters the complexion of things.'

A picture rose swiftly in Poirot's mind. A sullen face and a passionate voice saying, 'The money is mine. She wrote it down and so it shall be.' The legacy would not come as a surprise to Katrina—she knew about it beforehand.

'Item No. 2,' continued the voice of Inspector Sims. 'Nobody but K. handled that cachet.'

'You can be sure of that?'

'The girl herself doesn't deny it. What do you think of that?'

'Extremely interesting.'

'We only want one thing more—evidence of how the strychnine came into her possession. That oughtn't to be difficult.'

'But so far you haven't been successful?'

'I've barely started. The inquest was only this morning.'

'What happened at it?'

'Adjourned for a week.'

'And the young lady—K?'

'I'm detaining her on suspicion. Don't want to run any risks. She might have some funny friends in the country who'd try to get her out of it.'

'No,' said Poirot. 'I do not think she has any friends.'

'Really? What makes you say that, M. Poirot?'

'It is just an idea of mine. There were no other "items", as you call them?'

'Nothing that's strictly relevant. Miss B. seems to have been monkeying about a bit with her shares lately—must have dropped quite a tidy sum. It's rather a funny business, one way and another, but I don't see how it affects the main issue—not at present, that is.'

'No, perhaps you are right. Well, my best thanks to you. It was most amiable of you to ring me up.'

'Not at all. I'm a man of my word. I could see you were interested. Who knows, you may be able to give me a helping hand before the end.'

'That would give me great pleasure. It might help you, for instance, if I could lay my hand on a friend of the girl Katrina.'

'I thought you said she hadn't got any friends?' said Inspector Sims, surprised.

'I was wrong,' said Hercule Poirot. 'She has one.'

Before the inspector could ask a further question, Poirot had rung off.

With a serious face he wandered into the room where Miss Lemon sat at her typewriter. She raised her hands from the keys at her employer's approach and looked at him inquiringly.

'I want you,' said Poirot, 'to figure to yourself a little history.'

Miss Lemon dropped her hands into her lap in a resigned manner. She enjoyed typing, paying bills, filing papers and entering up engagements. To be asked to imagine herself in hypothetical situations bored her very much, but she accepted it as a disagreeable part of a duty.

'You are a Russian girl,' began Poirot.

'Yes,' said Miss Lemon, looking intensely British.

'You are alone and friendless in this country. You have reasons for not wishing to return to Russia. You are employed as a kind of drudge, nurse-attendant and companion to an old lady. You are meek and uncomplaining.'

'Yes,' said Miss Lemon obediently, but entirely failing to see herself being meek to any old lady under the sun.

'The old lady takes a fancy to you. She decides to leave her money to you. She tells you so.' Poirot paused.

Miss Lemon said 'Yes' again.

'And then the old lady finds out something; perhaps it is a matter of money—she may find that you have not been honest with her. Or it might be more grave still—a medicine that tasted different, some food that disagreed. Anyway, she begins to suspect you of something and she writes to a very famous detective—*enfin*, to the most famous detective—me! I am to call upon her shortly.

62

And then, as you say, the dripping will be in the fire. The great thing is to act quickly. And so—before the great detective arrives—the old lady is dead. And the money comes to you. . . Tell me, does that seem to you reasonable?'

'Quite reasonable,' said Miss Lemon. 'Quite reasonable for a Russian, that is. Personally, I should never take a post as a companion. I like my duties clearly defined. And of course I should not dream of murdering anyone.'

Poirot sighed. 'How I miss my friend Hastings. He had such imagination. Such a romantic mind! It is true that he always imagined wrong—but that in itself was a guide.'

Miss Lemon was silent. She looked longingly at the typewritten sheet in front of her.

'So it seems to you reasonable,' mused Poirot.

'Doesn't it to you?'

'I am almost afraid it does,' sighed Poirot.

The telephone rang and Miss Lemon went out of the room to answer it. She came back to say 'It's Inspector Sims again.' Poirot hurried to the instrument. ''Allo, 'allo. What is that you say?'

Sims repeated his statement. 'We've found a packet of strychnine in the girl's bedroom—tucked underneath the mattress. The sergeant's just come in with the news. That about clinches it, I think.'

'Yes,' said Poirot, 'I think that clinches it.' His voice had changed. It rang with sudden confidence.

When he had rung off, he sat down at his writing table and arranged the objects on it in a mechanical manner. He murmured to himself, 'There was something wrong. I felt it—no, not felt. It must have been something I saw. *En avant*, the little grey cells. Ponder—

63

reflect. Was everything logical and in order? The girl—her anxiety about the money: Mme Delafontaine; her husband—his suggestion of Russians—imbecile, but he is an imbecile; the room; the garden—ah! Yes, the garden.'

He sat up very stiff. The green light shone in his eyes. He sprang up and went into the adjoining room.

'Miss Lemon, will you have the kindness to leave what you are doing and make an investigation for me?'

'An investigation, M. Poirot? I'm afraid I'm not very good—'

Poirot interrupted her. 'You said one day that you knew all about tradesmen.'

'Certainly I do,' said Miss Lemon with confidence.

'Then the matter is simple. You are to go to Charman's Green and you are to discover a fishmonger.'

'A fishmonger?' asked Miss Lemon, surprised.

'Precisely. The fishmonger who supplied Rosebank with fish. When you have found him you will ask him a certain question.'

He handed her a slip of paper. Miss Lemon took it, noted its contents without interest, then nodded and slipped the lid on her typewriter.

'We will go to Charman's Green together,' said Poirot. 'You go to the fishmonger and I to the police station. It will take us but half an hour from Baker Street.'

On arrival at his destination, he was greeted by the surprised Inspector Sims. 'Well, this is quick work, M. Poirot. I was talking to you on the phone only an hour ago.'

'I have a request to make to you; that you allow me to see this girl Katrina—what is her name?'

'Katrina Rieger. Well, I don't suppose there's any objection to that.'

The girl Katrina looked even more sallow and sullen than ever.

Poirot spoke to her very gently. 'Mademoiselle, I want you to believe that I am not your enemy. I want you to tell me the truth.'

Her eyes snapped defiantly. 'I have told the truth. To everyone I have told the truth! If the old lady was poisoned, it was not I who poisoned her. It is all a mistake. You wish to prevent me having the money.' Her voice was rasping. She looked, he thought, like a miserable little cornered rat.

'Did no one handle it but you?'

'I have said so, have I not? They were made up at the chemist's that afternoon. I brought them back with me in my bag—that was just before supper. I opened the box and gave Miss Barrowby one with a glass of water.'

'No one touched them but you?'

'No.' A cornered rat—with courage!

'And Miss Barrowby had for supper only what we have been told. The soup, the fish pie, the tart?'

'Yes.' A hopeless 'yes'—dark, smouldering eyes that saw no light anywhere.

Poirot patted her shoulder. 'Be of good courage, mademoiselle. There may yet be freedom—yes, and money—a life of ease.'

She looked at him suspiciously.

As she went out Sims said to him, 'I didn't quite get what you said through the telephone—something about the girl having a friend.'

'She has one. Me!' said Hercule Poirot, and had left the police station before the inspector could pull his wits together.

★   ★   ★

65

At the Green Cat tearooms, Miss Lemon did not keep her employer waiting. She went straight to the point.

'The man's name is Rudge, in the High Street, and you were quite right. A dozen and a half exactly. I've made a note of what he said.' She handed it to him.

'Arrr.' It was a deep, rich sound like a purr of a cat.

Hercule Poirot betook himself to Rosebank. As he stood in the front garden, the sun setting behind him, Mary Delafontaine came out to him.

'M. Poirot?' Her voice sounded surprised. 'You have come back?'

'Yes, I have come back.' He paused and then said, 'When I first came here, madame, the children's nursery rhyme came into my head:

'Mistress Mary, quite contrary,
How does your garden grow?
With cockle-shells, and silver bells,
And pretty maids all in a row.

'Only they are not *cockle* shells, are they, madame? They are *oyster* shells.' His hand pointed.

He heard her catch her breath and then stay very still. Her eyes asked a question.

He nodded. '*Mais, oui*, I know! The maid left the dinner ready—she will swear and Katrina will swear that that is all you had. Only you and your husband know that you brought back a dozen and a half oysters—a little treat *pour la bonne tante*. So easy to put the strychnine in an oyster. It is swallowed—*comme ça*! But there remain the shells—they must not go in the bucket. The maid would see them. And so you thought of making an edging of them to a bed. But there were not enough—

the edging is not complete. The effect is bad—it spoils the symmetry of the otherwise charming garden. Those few oyster shells struck an alien note—they displeased my eye on my first visit.'

Mary Delafontaine said, 'I suppose you guessed from the letter. I knew she had written—but I didn't know how much she'd said.'

Poirot answered evasively, 'I knew at least that it was a family matter. If it had been a question of Katrina there would have been no point in hushing things up. I understand that you or your husband handled Miss Barrowby's securities to your own profit, and that she found out—'

Mary Delafontaine nodded. 'We've done it for years—a little here and there. I never realized she was sharp enough to find out. And then I learned she had sent for a detective; and I found out, too, that she was leaving her money to Katrina—that miserable little creature!'

'And so the strychnine was put in Katrina's bedroom? I comprehend. You save yourself and your husband from what I may discover, and you saddle an innocent child with murder. Had you no pity, madame?'

Mary Delafontaine shrugged her shoulders—her blue forget-me-not eyes looked into Poirot's. He remembered the perfection of her acting the first day he had come and the bungling attempts of her husband. A woman above the average—but inhuman.

She said, 'Pity? For that miserable intriguing little rat?' Her contempt rang out.

Hercule Poirot said slowly, 'I think, madame, that you have cared in your life for two things only. One is your husband.'

He saw her lips tremble.

'And the other—is your garden.'

He looked round him. His glance seemed to apologize to the flowers for that which he had done and was about to do.

Swan Song

It was eleven o'clock on a May morning in London. Mr Cowan was looking out of the window, behind him was the somewhat ornate splendour of a sitting-room in a suite at the Ritz Hotel. The suite in question had been reserved for Mme Paula Nazorkoff, the famous operatic star, who had just arrived in London. Mr Cowan, who was Madame's principal man of business, was awaiting an interview with the lady. He turned his head suddenly as the door opened, but it was only Miss Read, Mme Nazorkoff's secretary, a pale girl with an efficient manner.

'Oh, so it's you, my dear,' said Mr Cowan. 'Madame not up yet, eh?'

Miss Read shook her head.

'She told me to come round at ten o'clock,' Mr Cowan said. 'I have been waiting an hour.'

He displayed neither resentment nor surprise. Mr Cowan was indeed accustomed to the vagaries of the artistic temperament. He was a tall man, clean-shaven, with a frame rather too well covered, and clothes that were rather too faultless. His hair was very black and shining, and his teeth were aggressively white. When he spoke, he had a way of slurring his 's's' which was not quite a lisp, but came perilously near to it. It required no stretch of imagination to realize that his father's name had probably been Cohen. At that minute a door at the other side of the room opened, and a trim, French girl hurried through.

'Madame getting up?' inquired Cowan hopefully. 'Tell us the news, Elise.'

Elise immediately elevated both hands to heaven.

'Madame she is like seventeen devils this morning, nothing pleases her! The beautiful yellow roses which monsieur sent to her last night, she says they are all very well for New York, but that it is *imbecile* to send them to her in London. In London, she says, red roses are the only things possible, and straight away she opens the door, and precipitates the yellow roses into the passage, where they descend upon a monsieur, *très comme il faut*, a military gentleman, I think, and he is justly indignant, that one!'

Cowan raised his eyebrows, but displayed no other signs of emotion. Then he took from his pocket a small memorandum book and pencilled in it the words 'red roses'.

Elise hurried out through the other door, and Cowan turned once more to the window. Vera Read sat down at the desk, and began opening letters and sorting them. Ten minutes passed in silence, and then the door of the bedroom burst open, and Paula Nazorkoff flamed into the room. Her immediate effect upon it was to make it seem smaller, Vera Read appeared more colourless, and Cowan retreated into a mere figure in the background.

'Ah, ha! My children,' said the prima donna, 'am I not punctual?'

She was a tall woman, and for a singer not unduly fat. Her arms and legs were still slender, and her neck was a beautiful column. Her hair, which was coiled in a great roll half-way down her neck, was of a dark, glowing red. If it owed some at least of its colour to henna, the result was none the less effective. She was not a young woman, forty at least, but the lines of her face were still lovely, though the skin was loosened and wrinkled round the flashing, dark eyes. She had the laugh of a child, the digestion of an ostrich, and the temper of a fiend, and she was acknowledged to be the greatest dramatic soprano of her day. She turned directly upon Cowan.

'Have you done as I asked you? Have you taken that abominable English piano away, and thrown it into the Thames?'

'I have got another for you,' said Cowan, and gestured towards where it stood in the corner.

Nazorkoff rushed across to it, and lifted the lid.

'An Erard,' she said, 'that is better. Now let us see.'

The beautiful soprano voice rang out in an arpeggio, then it ran lightly up and down the scale twice, then took a soft little run up to a high note, held it, its volume swelling louder and louder, then softened again till it died away in nothingness.

'Ah!' said Paula Nazorkoff in naïve satisfaction. 'What a beautiful voice I have! Even in London I have a beautiful voice.'

'That is so,' agreed Cowan in hearty congratulation. 'And you bet London is going to fall for you all right, just as New York did.'

'You think so?' queried the singer.

There was a slight smile on her lips, and it was evident that for her the question was a mere commonplace.

'Sure thing,' said Cowan.

Paula Nazorkoff closed the piano lid down and walked across to the table, with that slow undulating walk that proved so effective on the stage.

'Well, well,' she said, 'let us get to business. You have all the arrangements there, my friend?'

Cowan took some papers out of the portfolio he had laid on a chair.

'Nothing has been altered much,' he remarked. 'You will sing five times at Covent Garden, three times in *Tosca*, twice in *Aida*.'

'*Aida*! Pah,' said the prima donna; 'it will be unutterable boredom. *Tosca*, that is different.'

'Ah, yes,' said Cowan. '*Tosca* is *your* part.'

Paula Nazorkoff drew herself up.

'I am the greatest Tosca in the world,' she said simply.

'That is so,' agreed Cowan. 'No one can touch you.'

'Roscari will sing "Scarpia", I suppose?'

Cowan nodded.

'And Emile Lippi.'

'What?' shrieked Nazorkoff. 'Lippi, that hideous little barking frog, croak—croak—croak. I will not sing with him, I will bite him, I will scratch his face.'

'Now, now,' said Cowan soothingly.

'He does not sing, I tell you, he is a mongrel dog who barks.'

'Well, we'll see, we'll see,' said Cowan.

He was too wise ever to argue with temperamental singers.

'The Cavardossi?' demanded Nazorkoff.

'The American tenor, Hensdale.'

The other nodded.

'He is a nice little boy, he sings prettily.'

'And Barrère is to sing it once, I believe.'

'He is an artist,' said Madame generously. 'But to let that croaking frog Lippi be Scarpia! Bah—I'll not sing with him.'

'You leave it to me,' said Cowan soothingly.

He cleared his throat, and took up a fresh set of papers.

'I am arranging for a special concert at the Albert Hall.'

Nazorkoff made a grimace.

'I know, I know,' said Cowan; 'but everybody does it.'

'I will be good,' said Nazorkoff, 'and it will be filled to the ceiling, and I shall have much money. *Ecco!*'

Again Cowan shuffled papers.

'Now here is quite a different proposition,' he said, 'from Lady Rustonbury. She wants you to go down and sing.'

'Rustonbury?'

The prima donna's brow contracted as if in the effort to recollect something.

'I have read that name lately, very lately. It is a town— or a village, isn't it?'

'That's right, pretty little place in Hertfordshire. As for Lord Rustonbury's place, Rustonbury Castle, it's a real dandy old feudal seat, ghosts and family pictures, and secret staircases, and a slap-up private theatre. Rolling in money they are, and always giving some private show. She suggests that we give a complete opera, preferably *Butterfly*.'

'*Butterfly?*'

Cowan nodded.

'And they are prepared to pay. We'll have to square Covent Garden, of course, but even after that it will be well worth your while financially. In all probability, royalty will be present. It will be a slap-up advertisement.'

Madame raised her still beautiful chin.

'Do I need advertisement?' she demanded proudly.

'You can't have too much of a good thing,' said Cowan, unabashed.

'Rustonbury,' murmured the singer, 'where did I see—?'

She sprang up suddenly, and running to the centre table, began turning over the pages of an illustrated paper which lay there. There was a sudden pause as her hand stopped, hovering over one of the pages, then she let the periodical slip to the floor and returned slowly to her seat. With one of her swift changes of mood, she seemed now an entirely different personality. Her manner was very quiet, almost austere.

'Make all arrangements for Rustonbury, I would like to sing there, but there is one condition—the opera must be *Tosca*.'

Cowan looked doubtful.

'That will be rather difficult—for a private show, you know, scenery and all that.'

'*Tosca* or nothing.'

Cowan looked at her very closely. What he saw seemed to convince him, he gave a brief nod and rose to his feet.

'I will see what I can arrange,' he said quietly.

Nazorkoff rose too. She seemed more anxious than was usual, with her, to explain her decision.

'It is my greatest rôle, Cowan. I can sing that part as no other woman has ever sung it.'

'It is a fine part,' said Cowan. 'Jeritza made a great hit in it last year.'

'Jeritza!' cried the other, a flush mounting in her cheeks. She proceeded to give him at great length her opinion of Jeritza.

Cowan, who was used to listening to singers' opinions of other singers, abstracted his attention till the tirade was over; he then said obstinately:

'Anyway, she sings "Vissi D'Arte" lying on her stomach.'

'And why not?' demanded Nazorkoff. 'What is there to prevent her? I will sing it on my back with my legs waving in the air.'

Cowan shook his head with perfect seriousness.

'I don't believe that would go down any,' he informed her. 'All the same, that sort of thing takes on, you know.'

'No one can sing "Vissi D'Arte" as I can,' said Nazorkoff confidently. 'I sing it in the voice of the convent—as the good nuns taught me to sing years and years ago. In the voice of a choir boy or an angel, without feeling, without passion.'

'I know,' said Cowan heartily. 'I have heard you, you are wonderful.'

'That is art,' said the prima donna, 'to pay the price, to suffer, to endure, and in the end not only to have all knowledge, but also the power to go back, right back to the beginning and recapture the lost beauty of the heart of a child.'

Cowan looked at her curiously. She was staring past him with a strange, blank look in her eyes, and something about that look of hers gave him a creepy feeling. Her lips just parted, and she whispered a few words softly to herself. He only just caught them.

'At last,' she murmured. 'At last—*after all these years.*'

Lady Rustonbury was both an ambitious and an artistic woman, she ran the two qualities in harness with complete success. She had the good fortune to have a husband who cared for neither ambition nor art and who therefore did not hamper her in any way. The Earl of Rustonbury was a large, square man, with an interest in horseflesh and in nothing else. He admired his wife, and was proud of her, and was glad that his great wealth enabled her to indulge all her schemes. The private theatre had been built less than a hundred years ago by his grandfather. It was Lady Rustonbury's chief toy— she had already given an Ibsen drama in it, and a play of the ultra new school, all divorce and drugs, also a poetical fantasy with Cubist scenery. The forthcoming performance of *Tosca* had created wide-spread interest. Lady Rustonbury was entertaining a very distinguished houseparty for it, and all London that counted was motoring down to attend.

Mme Nazorkoff and her company had arrived just before luncheon. The new young American tenor, Hensdale, was to sing 'Cavaradossi', and Roscari, the famous Italian baritone, was to be Scarpia. The expense of the production had been enormous, but nobody cared about that. Paula Nazorkoff was in the best of humours, she was charming, gracious, her most delightful and cosmopolitan self. Cowan was agreeably surprised, and prayed that this state of things might continue.

After luncheon the company went out to the theatre, and inspected the scenery and various appointments. The orchestra was under the direction of Mr Samuel Ridge, one of England's most famous conductors. Everything seemed to be going without a hitch, and strangely enough, that fact worried Mr Cowan. He was more at home in an atmosphere of trouble, this unusual peace disturbed him.

'Everything is going a darned sight too smoothly,' murmured Mr Cowan to himself. 'Madame is like a cat that has been fed on cream, it's too good to last, something is bound to happen.'

Perhaps as the result of his long contact with the operatic world, Mr Cowan had developed the sixth sense, certainly his prognostications were justified. It was just before seven o'clock that evening when the

French maid, Elise, came running to him in great distress.

'Ah, Mr Cowan, come quickly, I beg of you come quickly.'

'What's the matter?' demanded Cowan anxiously. 'Madame got her back up about anything—ructions, eh, is that it?'

'No, no, it is not Madame, it is Signor Roscari, he is ill, he is dying!'

'Dying? Oh, come now.'

Cowan hurried after her as she led the way to the stricken Italian's bedroom. The little man was lying on his bed, or rather jerking himself all over it in a series of contortions that would have been humorous had they been less grave. Paula Nazorkoff was bending over him; she greeted Cowan imperiously.

'Ah! there you are. Our poor Roscari, he suffers horribly. Doubtless he has eaten something.'

'I am dying,' groaned the little man. 'The pain—it is terrible. Ow!'

He contorted himself again, clasping both hands to his stomach, and rolling about on the bed.

'We must send for a doctor,' said Cowan.

Paula arrested him as he was about to move to the door.

'The doctor is already on his way, he will do all that can be done for the poor suffering one, that is arranged for, but never never will Roscari be able to sing tonight.'

'I shall never sing again, I am dying,' groaned the Italian.

'No, no, you are not dying,' said Paula. 'It is but an indigestion, but all the same, impossible that you should sing.'

'I have been poisoned.'

'Yes, it is the ptomaine without doubt,' said Paula. 'Stay with him, Elise, till the doctor comes.'

The singer swept Cowan with her from the room.

'What are we to do?' she demanded.

Cowan shook his head hopelessly. The hour was so far advanced that it would not be possible to get anyone from London to take Roscari's place. Lady Rustonbury, who had just been informed of her guest's illness, came hurrying along the corridor to join them. Her principal concern, like Paula Nazorkoff's, was the success of *Tosca*.

'If there were only someone near at hand,' groaned the prima donna.

'Ah!' Lady Rustonbury gave a sudden cry. 'Of course! Bréon.'

'Bréon?'

'Yes, Edouard Bréon, you know, the famous French baritone. He lives near here, there was a picture of his house in this week's *Country Homes*. He is the very man.'

'It is an answer from heaven,' cried Nazorkoff. 'Bréon as Scarpia, I remember him well, it was one of his greatest rôles. But he has retired, has he not?'

'I will get him,' said Lady Rustonbury. 'Leave it to me.'

And being a woman of decision, she straightway ordered out the *Hispano Suiza*. Ten minutes later, M. Edouard Bréon's country retreat was invaded by an agitated countess. Lady Rustonbury, once she had made her mind up, was a very determined woman, and doubtless M. Bréon realized that there was nothing for it but to submit. Himself a man of very humble origin, he had climbed to the top of his profession, and had consorted on equal terms with dukes and princes, and the fact never failed to gratify him. Yet, since his retirement to this old-world English spot, he had known discontent.

He missed the life of adulation and applause, and the English county had not been as prompt to recognize him as he thought they should have been. So he was greatly flattered and charmed by Lady Rustonbury's request.

'I will do my poor best,' he said, smiling. 'As you know, I have not sung in public for a long time now. I do not even take pupils, only one or two as a great favour. But there—since Signor Roscari is unfortunately indisposed—'

'It was a terrible blow,' said Lady Rustonbury.

'Not that he is really a singer,' said Bréon.

He told her at some length why this was so. There had been, it seemed, no baritone of distinction since Edouard Bréon retired.

'Mme Nazorkoff is singing "Tosca",' said Lady Rustonbury. 'You know her, I dare say?'

'I have never met her,' said Bréon. 'I heard her sing once in New York. A great artist—she has a sense of drama.'

Lady Rustonbury felt relieved—one never knew with these singers—they had such queer jealousies and antipathies.

She re-entered the hall at the castle some twenty minutes later waving a triumphant hand.

'I have got him,' she cried, laughing. 'Dear M. Bréon has really been too kind, I shall never forget it.'

Everyone crowded round the Frenchman, and their gratitude and appreciation were as incense to him. Edouard Bréon, though now close on sixty, was still a fine-looking man, big and dark, with a magnetic personality.

'Let me see,' said Lady Rustonbury. 'Where is Madame—? Oh! there she is.'

Paula Nazorkoff had taken no part in the general welcoming of the Frenchman. She had remained quietly sitting in a high oak chair in the shadow of the fireplace. There was, of course, no fire, for the evening was a warm one and the singer was slowly fanning herself with an immense palm-leaf fan. So aloof and detached was she, that Lady Rustonbury feared she had taken offence.

'M. Bréon.' She led him up to the singer. 'You have never yet met Madame Nazorkoff, you say.'

With a last wave, almost a flourish, of the palm leaf, Paula Nazorkoff laid it down, and stretched out her hand to the Frenchman. He took it and bowed low over it, and a faint sigh escaped from the prima donna's lips.

'Madame,' said Bréon, 'we have never sung together. That is the penalty of my age! But Fate has been kind to me, and come to my rescue.'

Paula laughed softly.

'You are too kind, M. Bréon. When I was still but a poor little unknown singer, I have sat at your feet. Your "Rigoletto"—what art, what perfection! No one could touch you.'

'Alas!' said Bréon, pretending to sigh. 'My day is over. Scarpia, Rigoletto, Radames, Sharpless, how many times have I not sung them, and now—no more!'

'Yes—tonight.'

'True, Madame—I forgot. Tonight.'

'You have sung with many "Toscas",' said Nazorkoff arrogantly; 'but never with *me*!'

The Frenchman bowed.

'It will be an honour,' he said softly. 'It is a great part, Madame.'

'It needs not only a singer, but an actress,' put in Lady Rustonbury.

'That is true,' Bréon agreed. 'I remember when I was a young man in Italy, going to a little out of the way theatre in Milan. My seat cost me only a couple of lira, but I heard as good singing that night as I have heard in the Metropolitan Opera House in New York. Quite a young girl sang "Tosca", she sang it like an angel. Never shall I forget her voice in "Vissi D'Arte", the clearness of it, the purity. But the dramatic force, that was lacking.'

Nazorkoff nodded.

'That comes later,' she said quietly.

'True. This young girl—Bianca Capelli, her name was—I interested myself in her career. Through me she had the chance of big engagements, but she was foolish—regrettably foolish.'

He shrugged his shoulders.

'How was she foolish?'

It was Lady Rustonbury's twenty-four-year-old daughter, Blanche Amery, who spoke. A slender girl with wide blue eyes.

The Frenchman turned to her at once politely.

'Alas! Mademoiselle, she had embroiled herself with some low fellow, a ruffian, a member of the Camorra. He got into trouble with the police, was condemned to death; she came to me begging me to do something to save her lover.'

Blanche Amery was staring at him.

'And did you?' she asked breathlessly.

'Me, Mademoiselle, what could I do? A stranger in the country.'

'You might have had influence?' suggested Nazorkoff, in her low vibrant voice.

'If I had, I doubt whether I should have exerted it. The man was not worth it. I did what I could for the girl.'

He smiled a little, and his smile suddenly struck the English girl as having something peculiarly disagreeable about it. She felt that, at that moment, his words fell far short of representing his thoughts.

'You did what you could,' said Nazorkoff. 'That was kind of you, and she was grateful, eh?'

The Frenchman shrugged his shoulders.

'The man was executed,' he said, 'and the girl entered a convent. Eh, *voilà!* The world has lost a singer.'

Nazorkoff gave a low laugh.

'We Russians are more fickle,' she said lightly.

Blanche Amery happened to be watching Cowan just as the singer spoke, and she saw his quick look of astonishment, and his lips that half-opened and then shut tight in obedience to some warning glance from Paula.

The butler appeared in the doorway.

'Dinner,' said Lady Rustonbury, rising. 'You poor things, I am so sorry for you, it must be dreadful always to have to starve yourself before singing. But there will be a very good supper afterwards.'

'We shall look forward to it,' said Paula Nazorkoff. She laughed softly. *'Afterwards!'*

Inside the theatre, the first act of *Tosca* had just drawn to a close. The audience stirred, spoke to each other. The royalties, charming and gracious, sat in the three velvet chairs in the front row. Everyone was whispering and murmuring to each other, there was a general feeling that in the first act Nazorkoff had hardly lived up to her great reputation. Most of the audience did not realize that in this the singer showed her art, in the first act she was saving her voice and herself. She made of La Tosca a light, frivolous figure, toying with love, coquettishly jealous and exciting. Bréon, though the glory of his voice was past its prime, still struck a magnificent figure as the cynical Scarpia. There was no hint of the decrepit roué in his conception of the part. He made of Scarpia a handsome, almost benign figure, with just a hint of the subtle malevolence that underlay the outward seeming. In the last passage, with the organ and the procession, when Scarpia stands lost in thought, gloating over his plan to secure Tosca, Bréon had displayed a wonderful art. Now the curtain rose up on the second act, the scene in Scarpia's apartments.

This time, when Tosca entered, the art of Nazorkoff at once became apparent. Here was a woman in deadly terror playing her part with the assurance of a fine actress. Her easy greeting of Scarpia, her nonchalance, her smiling replies to him! In this scene, Paula Nazorkoff acted with her eyes, she carried herself with deadly quietness, with an impassive, smiling face. Only her eyes that kept darting glances at Scarpia betrayed her true feelings. And so the story went on, the torture scene, the breaking down of Tosca's composure, and her utter abandonment when she fell at Scarpia's feet imploring him vainly for mercy. Old Lord Leconmere, a connoisseur of music, moved appreciatively, and a foreign ambassador sitting next to him murmured:

'She surpasses herself, Nazorkoff, tonight. There is no other woman on the stage who can let herself go as she does.'

Leconmere nodded.

And now Scarpia has named his price, and Tosca, horrified, flies from him to the window. Then comes the beat of drums from afar, and Tosca flings herself wearily down on the sofa. Scarpia standing over her, recites how his people are raising up the gallows—and then silence, and again the far-off beat of drums. Nazorkoff lay prone on the sofa, her head hanging downwards almost touching the floor, masked by her hair. Then, in exquisite contrast to the passion and stress of the last twenty minutes, her voice rang out, high and clear, the voice, as she had told Cowan, of a choir boy or an angel.

'Vissi d'arte, vissi d'arte, no feci mai male ad anima viva. Con man furtiva quante miserie conobbi, aiutai.'

It was the voice of a wondering, puzzled child. Then she is once more kneeling and imploring, till the instant when Spoletta enters. Tosca, exhausted, gives in, and Scarpia utters his fateful words of double-edged meaning. Spoletta departs once more. Then comes the dramatic moment, whe Tosca, raising a glass of wine in her trembling hand, catches sight of the knife on the table, and slips it behind her.

Bréon rose up, handsome, saturnine, inflamed with passion. *'Tosca, finalmente mia!'* The lightning stabs with the knife, and Tosca's hiss of vengeance:

'Questo e il bacio di Tosca!' ('It is thus that Tosca kisses.')

Never had Nazorkoff shown such an appreciation of Tosca's act of vengeance. That last fierce whispered *'Muori dannato,'* and then in a strange, quiet voice that filled the theatre:

'Or gli perdono!' ('Now I forgive him!')

The soft death tune began as Tosca set about her ceremonial, placing the candles each side of his head, the crucifix on his breast, her last pause in the doorway looking back, the roll of distant drums, and the curtain fell.

This time real enthusiasm broke out in the audience, but it was short-lived. Someone hurried out from behind the wings, and spoke to Lord Rustonbury. He rose, and after a minute or two's consultation, turned and beckoned to Sir Donald Calthorp, who was an eminent physician. Almost immediately the truth spread through the audience. Something had happened, an accident, someone was badly hurt. One of the singers appeared before the curtain and explained that M Bréon had unfortunately met with an accident—the opera could not proceed. Again the rumour went round, Bréon had been stabbed, Nazorkoff had lost her head, she had lived in her part so completely that she had actually stabbed the man who was acting with her. Lord Leconmere, talking to his ambassador friend, felt a touch on his arm, and turned to look into Blanche Amery's eyes.

'It was not an accident,' the girl was saying. 'I am sure it was not an accident. Didn't you hear, just before dinner, that story he was telling about the girl in Italy? That girl was Paula Nazorkoff. Just after, she said something about being Russian, and I saw Mr Cowan look amazed. She may have taken a Russian name, but he knows well enough that she is Italian.'

'My dear Blanche,' said Lord Leconmere.

'I tell you I am sure of it. She had a picture paper in her bedroom opened at the page showing M Bréon in his English country home. She knew before she came down here. I believe she gave something to that poor little Italian man to make him ill.'

'But why?' cried Lord Leconmere. 'Why?'

'Don't you see? It's the story of Tosca all over again. He wanted her in Italy, but she was faithful to her lover, and she went to him to try to get him to save her lover, and he pretended he would. Instead he let him die. And now at last her revenge has come. Didn't you hear the way she hissed "*I am Tosca*"? And I saw Bréon's face when she said it, *he knew then*—he recognized her!'

In her dressing-room, Paula Nazorkoff sat motionless,

a white ermine cloak held round her. There was a knock at the door.

'Come in,' said the prima donna.

Elise entered. She was sobbing.

'Madame, Madame, he is dead! And—'

'Yes?'

'Madame, how can I tell you? There are two gentlemen of the police there, they want to speak to you.'

Paula Nazorkoff rose to her full height.

'I will go to them,' she said quietly.

She untwisted a collar of pearls from her neck, and put them into the French girl's hands.

'Those are for you, Elise, you have been a good girl. I shall not need them now where I am going. You understand, Elise? *I shall not sing "Tosca" again.*'

She stood a moment by the door, her eyes sweeping over the dressing-room, as though she looked back over the past thirty years of her career.

Then softly between her teeth, she murmured the last line of another opera:

'*La commedia e finita!*'

Miss Marple Tells a Story

I don't think I've ever told you, my dears—you, Raymond, and you, Joan, about the rather curious little business that happened some years ago now. I don't want to seem *vain* in any way—of course I know that in comparison with you young people I'm not clever at all—Raymond writes those very modern books all about rather unpleasant young men and women—and Joan paints those very remarkable pictures of square people with curious bulges on them—very clever of you, my dear, but as Raymond always says (only quite kindly, because he is the kindest of nephews) I am hopelessly Victorian. I admire Mr Alma-Tadema and Mr Frederic Leighton and I suppose to you they seem hopelessly *vieux jeu*. Now let me see, what was I saying? Oh, yes—that I didn't want to appear vain—but I couldn't help being just a teeny weeny bit pleased with myself, because, just by applying a little common sense, I believe I really did solve a problem that had baffled cleverer heads than mine. Though really I should have thought the whole thing was *obvious* from the beginning . . .

Well, I'll tell you my little story, and if you think I'm inclined to be conceited about it, you must remember that I did at least help a fellow creature who was in very grave distress.

The first I knew of this business was one evening

about nine o'clock when Gwen—(you remember Gwen? My little maid with red hair) well—Gwen came in and told me that Mr Petherick and a gentleman had called to see me. Gwen had shown them into the drawing-room— quite rightly. I was sitting in the dining-room because in early spring I think it is so wasteful to have two fires going.

I directed Gwen to bring in the cherry brandy and some glasses and I hurried into the drawing-room. I don't know whether you remember Mr Petherick? He died two years ago, but he had been a friend of mine for many years as well as attending to all my legal business. A very shrewd man and a really clever solicitor. His son does my business for me now—a very nice lad and very up to date—but somehow I don't feel quite the *confidence* I had with Mr Petherick.

I explained to Mr Petherick about the fires and he said at once that he and his friend would come into the dining-room—and then he introduced his friend—a Mr Rhodes. He was a youngish man—not much over forty—and I saw at once there was something very wrong. His manner was most *peculiar*. One might have called it *rude* if one hadn't realized that the poor fellow was suffering from *strain*.

When we were settled in the dining-room and Gwen had brought the cherry brandy, Mr Petherick explained the reason for his visit.

'Miss Marple,' he said, 'you must forgive an old friend for taking a liberty. What I have come here for is a consultation.'

I couldn't understand at all what he meant, and he went on:

'In a case of illness one likes two points of view—that of the specialist and that of the family physician. It is the fashion to regard the former as of more value, but I am not sure that I agree. The specialist has experience only in his own subject—the family doctor has, perhaps, less knowledge—but a wider experience.'

I knew just what he meant, because a young niece of mine not long before had hurried her child off to a very well-known specialist in skin diseases without consulting her own doctor whom she considered an old dodderer, and the specialist had ordered some very expensive treatment, and later found that all the child was suffering from was a rather unusual form of measles.

I just mention this—though I have a horror of *digressing*—to show that I appreciate Mr Petherick's point—but I still hadn't any idea what he was driving at.

'If Mr Rhodes is ill—' I said, and stopped—because the poor man gave a most dreadful laugh.

He said: 'I expect to die of a broken neck in a few months' time.'

And then it all came out. There had been a case of murder lately in Barnchester—a town about twenty miles away. I'm afraid I hadn't paid much attention to it at the time, because we had been having a lot of excitement in the village about our district nurse, and outside occurrences like an earthquake in India and a murder in Barnchester, although of course far more important really—had given way to our own little local excitements. I'm afraid villages are like that. Still, I *did* remember having read about a woman having been stabbed in a hotel, though I hadn't remembered her name. But now it seemed that this woman had been Mr Rhodes's wife—and as if that wasn't bad enough—he was actually under suspicion of having murdered her himself.

All this Mr Petherick explained to me very clearly,

saying that, although the Coronor's jury had brought in a verdict of murder by a person or persons unknown, Mr Rhodes had reason to believe that he would probably be arrested within a day or two, and that he had come to Mr Petherick and placed himself in his hands. Mr Petherick went on to say that they had that afternoon consulted Sir Malcolm Olde, K.C., and that in the event of the case coming to trial Sir Malcolm had been briefed to defend Mr Rhodes.

Sir Malcolm was a young man, Mr Petherick said, very up to date in his methods, and he had indicated a certain line of defence. But with that line of defence Mr Petherick was not entirely satisfied.

'You see, my dear lady,' he said, 'it is tainted with what I call the specialist's point of view. Give Sir Malcolm a case and he sees only one point—the most likely line of defence. But even the best line of defence may ignore completely what is, to my mind, the vital point. It takes no account of what actually happened.'

Then he went on to say some very kind and flattering things about my acumen and judgement and my knowledge of human nature, and asked permission to tell me the story of the case in the hopes that I might be able to suggest some explanation.

I could see that Mr Rhodes was highly sceptical of my being of any use and he was annoyed at being brought here. But Mr Petherick took no notice and proceeded to give me the facts of what occurred on the night of March 8th.

Mr and Mrs Rhodes had been staying at the Crown Hotel in Barnchester. Mrs Rhodes who (so I gathered from Mr Petherick's careful language) was perhaps just a shade of a hypochondriac, had retired to bed immediately after dinner. She and her husband occupied

90

adjoining rooms with a connecting door. Mr Rhodes, who is writing a book on prehistoric flints, settled down to work in the adjoining room. At eleven o'clock he tidied up his papers and prepared to go to bed. Before doing so, he just glanced into his wife's room to make sure that there was nothing she wanted. He discovered the electric light on and his wife lying in bed stabbed through the heart. She had been dead at least an hour—probably longer. The following were the points made. There was another door in Mrs Rhodes's room leading into the corridor. This door was locked and bolted on the inside. The only window in the room was closed and latched. According to Mr Rhodes nobody had passed through the room in which he was sitting except a chambermaid bringing hot-water bottles. The weapon found in the wound was a stiletto dagger which had been lying on Mrs Rhodes's dressing-table. She was in the habit of using it as a paper knife. There were no fingerprints on it.

The situation boiled down to this—no one but Mr Rhodes and the chambermaid had entered the victim's room.

I enquired about the chambermaid.

'That was our first line of enquiry,' said Mr Petherick. 'Mary Hill is a local woman. She had been chambermaid at the Crown for ten years. There seems absolutely no reason why she should commit a sudden assault on a guest. She is, in any case, extraordinarily stupid, almost half-witted. Her story has never varied. She brought Mrs Rhodes her hot-water bottle and says the lady was drowsy—just dropping off to sleep. Frankly, I cannot believe, and I am sure no jury would believe, that she committed the crime.'

Mr Petherick went on to mention a few additional

details. At the head of the staircase in the Crown Hotel is a kind of miniature lounge where people sometimes sit and have coffee. A passage goes off to the right and the last door in it is the door into the room occupied by Mr Rhodes. The passage then turns sharply to the right again and the first door round the corner is the door into Mrs Rhodes's room. As it happened, both these doors could be seen by witnesses. The first door— that into Mr Rhodes's room, which I will call A, could be seen by four people, two commercial travellers and an elderly married couple who were having coffee. According to them nobody went in or out of door A except Mr Rhodes and the chambermaid. As to the other door in the passage B, there was an electrician at work there and he also swears that nobody entered or left door B except the chambermaid.

It was certainly a very curious and interesting case. On the face of it, it looked as though Mr Rhodes *must* have murdered his wife. But I could see that Mr Petherick was quite convinced of his client's innocence and Mr Petherick was a very shrewd man.

At the inquest Mr Rhodes had told a hesitating and rambling story about some woman who had written threatening letters to his wife. His story, I gathered, had been unconvincing in the extreme. Appealed to by Mr Petherick, he explained himself.

'Frankly,' he said, 'I never believed it. I thought Amy had made most of it up.'

Mrs Rhodes, I gathered, was one of those romantic liars who go through life embroidering everything that happens to them. The amount of adventures that, according to her own account, happened to her in a year was simply incredible. If she slipped on a bit of banana peel it was a case of near escape from death. If a lampshade caught fire she was rescued from a burning building at the hazard of her life. Her husband got into the habit of discounting her statements. Her tale as to some woman whose child she had injured in a motor accident and who had vowed vengeance on her—well—Mr Rhodes had simply not taken any notice of it. The incident had happened before he married his wife and although she had read him letters couched in crazy language, he had suspected her of composing them herself. She had actually done such a thing once or twice before. She was a woman of hysterical tendencies who craved ceaselessly for excitement.

Now, all that seemed to me very natural—indeed, we have a young woman in the village who does much the same thing. The danger with such people is that when anything at all extraordinary really does happen to them, nobody believes they are speaking the truth. It seemed to me that that was what had happened in this case. The police, I gathered, merely believed that Mr Rhodes was making up this unconvincing tale in order to avert suspicion from himself.

I asked if there had been any women staying by themselves in the hotel. It seemed there were two—a Mrs Granby, an Anglo-Indian widow, and a Miss Carruthers, rather a horsey spinster who dropped her g's. Mr Petherick added that the most minute enquiries had failed to elicit anyone who had seen either of them near the scene of the crime and there was nothing to connect either of them with it in any way. I asked him to describe their personal appearance. He said that Mrs Granby had reddish hair rather untidily done, was sallow-faced and about fifty years of age. Her clothes were rather picturesque, being made mostly of native silk, etc. Miss Carruthers was about forty, wore pince-nez, had close-cropped hair like a man and wore mannish coats and skirts.

'Dear me,' I said, 'that makes it very difficult.'

Mr Petherick looked enquiringly at me, but I didn't want to say any more just then, so I asked what Sir Malcolm Olde had said.

Sir Malcolm was confident of being able to call conflicting medical testimony and to suggest some way of getting over the fingerprint difficulty. I asked Mr Rhodes what he thought and he said all doctors were fools but he himself couldn't really believe that his wife had killed herself. 'She wasn't that kind of woman,' he said simply—and I believed him. Hysterical people don't usually commit suicide.

I thought a minute and then I asked if the door from Mrs Rhodes's room led straight into the corridor. Mr Rhodes said no—there was a little hallway with a bathroom and lavatory. It was the door from the bedroom to the hallway that was locked and bolted on the inside.

'In that case,' I said, 'the whole thing seems remarkably simple.'

And really, you know, it *did* ... the simplest thing in the world. And yet no one seemed to have seen it that way.

Both Mr Petherick and Mr Rhodes were staring at me so that I felt quite embarrassed.

'Perhaps,' said Mr Rhodes, 'Miss Marple hasn't quite appreciated the difficulties.'

'Yes,' I said, 'I think I have. There are four possibilities. Either Mrs Rhodes was killed by her husband, or by the chambermaid, or she committed suicide, or she was killed by an outsider whom nobody saw enter or leave.'

'And that's impossible,' Mr Rhodes broke in. 'Nobody could come in or go out through my room without my seeing them, and even if anyone did manage to come in through my wife's room without the electrician seeing them, how the devil could they get out again leaving the door locked and bolted on the inside?'

Mr Petherick looked at me and said: 'Well, Miss Marple?' in an encouraging manner.

'I should like,' I said, 'to ask a question. Mr Rhodes, what did the chambermaid look like?'

He said he wasn't sure—she was tallish, he thought—he didn't remember if she was fair or dark. I turned to Mr Petherick and asked the same question.

He said she was of medium height, had fairish hair and blue eyes and rather a high colour.

Mr Rhodes said: 'You are a better observer than I am, Petherick.'

I ventured to disagree. I then asked Mr Rhodes if he could describe the maid in my house. Neither he nor Mr Petherick could do so.

'Don't you see what that means?' I said. 'You both came here full of your own affairs and the person who let you in was only a *parlourmaid*. The same applies to Mr Rhodes at the hotel. He saw her uniform and her apron. He was engrossed by his work. But Mr Petherick has interviewed the same woman in a different capacity. He has looked at her as a *person*.

'That's what the woman who did the murder counted upon.'

As they still didn't see, I had to explain.

'I think,' I said, 'that this is how it went. The chambermaid came in by door A, passed through Mr Rhodes's room into Mrs Rhodes's room with the hot-water bottle and went out through the hallway into passage B. X—as

I will call our murderess—came in by door B into the little hallway, concealed herself in—well, in a certain apartment, ahem—and waited until the chambermaid had passed out. Then she entered Mrs Rhodes's room, took the stiletto from the dressing table (she had doubtless explored the room earlier in the day), went up to the bed, stabbed the dozing woman, wiped the handle of the stiletto, locked and bolted the door by which she had entered, and then passed out through the room where Mr Rhodes was working.'

Mr Rhodes cried out: 'But I should have *seen* her. The electrician would have seen her go in.'

'No,' I said. 'That's where you're wrong. You wouldn't see her—*not if she were dressed as a chambermaid.*' I let it sink in, then I went on, 'You were engrossed in your work—out of the tail of your eye you saw a chambermaid come in, go into your wife's room, come back and go out. It was the same *dress*—but not the same woman. That's what the people having coffee saw—a chambermaid go in and a chambermaid come out. The electrician did the same. I dare say if a chambermaid were very pretty a gentleman might notice her face—human nature being what it is—but if she were just an ordinary middle-aged woman—well—it would be the chambermaid's *dress* you would see—not the woman herself.'

Mr Rhodes cried: 'Who was she?'

'Well,' I said, 'that is going to be a little difficult. It must be either Mrs Granby or Miss Carruthers. Mrs Granby sounds as though she might wear a wig normally—so she could wear her own hair as a chambermaid. On the other hand, Miss Carruthers with her close-cropped mannish head might easily put on a wig to play her part. I dare say you will find out easily enough which of them it is. Personally, I incline myself to think it will be Miss Carruthers.'

And really, my dears, that is the end of the story. Carruthers was a false name, but she was the woman all right. There was insanity in her family. Mrs Rhodes, who was a most reckless and dangerous driver, had run over her little girl, and it had driven the poor woman off her head. She concealed her madness very cunningly except for writing distinctly insane latters to her intended victim. She had been following her about for some time, and she laid her plans very cleverly. The false hair and maid's dress she posted in a parcel first thing the next morning. When taxed with the truth she broke down and confessed at once. The poor thing is in Broadmoor now. Completely unbalanced of course, but a very cleverly planned crime.

Mr Petherick came to me afterwards and brought me a very nice letter from Mr Rhodes—really, it made me blush. Then my old friend said to me: 'Just one thing— why did you think it was more likely to be Carruthers than Granby? You'd never seen either of them.'

'Well,' I said. 'It was the g's. You said she dropped her g's. Now, that's done by a lot of hunting people in books, but I don't know many people who do it in reality—and certainly no one under sixty. You said this woman was forty. Those dropped g's sounded to me like a woman who was playing a part and over-doing it.'

I shan't tell you what Mr Petherick said to that—but he was very complimentary—and I really couldn't help feeling just a teeny weeny bit pleased with myself.

And it's extraordinary how things turn out for the best in this world. Mr Rhodes has married again— such a nice, sensible girl—and they've got a dear little baby and—what do you think?—they asked me to be godmother. Wasn't it nice of them?

Now I do hope you don't think I've been running on too long . . .

Have You Got Everything You Want?

'*Par ici, Madame.*'

A tall woman in a mink coat followed her heavily encumbered porter along the platform of the Gare de Lyon.

She wore a dark-brown knitted hat pulled down over one eye and ear. The other side revealed a charming tip-tilted profile and little golden curls clustering over a shell-like ear. Typically an American, she was altogether a very charming-looking creature and more than one man turned to look at her as she walked past the high carriages of the waiting train.

Large plates were stuck in holders on the sides of the carriages.

PARIS–ATHENES. PARIS–BUCHAREST.
PARIS–STAMBOUL.

At the last named the porter came to an abrupt halt. He undid the strap which held the suitcases together and they slipped heavily to the ground. '*Voici, Madame.*'

The *wagon-lit* conductor was standing beside the steps. He came forward, remarking, '*Bonsoir, Madame,*' with an *empressement* perhaps due to the richness and perfection of the mink coat.

The woman handed him her sleeping-car ticket of flimsy paper.

'Number Six,' he said. 'This way.'

He sprang nimbly into the train, the woman following him. As she hurried down the corridor after him, she nearly collided with a portly gentleman who was emerging from the compartment next to hers. She had a momentary glimpse of a large bland face with benevolent eyes.

'*Voici, Madame.*'

The conductor displayed the compartment. He threw up the window and signalled to the porter. The lesser employee took in the baggage and put it up on the racks. The woman sat down.

Beside her on the seat she had placed a small scarlet case and her handbag. The carriage was hot, but it did not seem to occur to her to take off her coat. She stared out of the window with unseeing eyes. People were hurrying up and down the platform. There were sellers of newspapers, of pillows, of chocolate, of fruit, of mineral waters. They held up their wares to her, but her eyes looked blankly through them. The Gare de Lyon had faded from her sight. On her face were sadness and anxiety.

'If Madame will give me her passport?'

The words made no impression on her. The conductor, standing in the doorway, repeated them. Elsie Jeffries roused herself with a start.

'I beg your pardon?'

'Your passport, Madame.'

She opened her bag, took out the passport and gave it to him.

'That will be all right, Madame, I will attend to everything.' A slight significant pause. 'I shall be going with Madame as far as Stamboul.'

Elsie drew out a fifty-franc note and handed it to

him. He accepted it in a business-like manner, and inquired when she would like her bed made up and whether she was taking dinner.

These matters settled, he withdrew and almost immediately the restaurant man came rushing down the corridor ringing his little bell frantically, and bawling out, '*Premier service. Premier service.*'

Elsie rose, divested herself of the heavy fur coat, took a brief glance at herself in the little mirror, and picking up her handbag and jewel case stepped out into the corridor. She had gone only a few steps when the restaurant man came rushing along on his return journey. To avoid him, Elsie stepped back for a moment into the doorway of the adjoining compartment, which was now empty. As the man passed and she prepared to continue her journey to the dining car, her glance fell idly on the label of a suitcase which was lying on the seat.

It was a stout pigskin case, somewhat worn. On the label were the words: 'J. Parker Pyne, passenger to Stamboul.' The suitcase itself bore the initials 'P.P.'

A startled expression came over the girl's face. She hesitated a moment in the corridor, then going back to her own compartment she picked up a copy of *The Times* which she had laid down on the table with some magazines and books.

She ran her eye down the advertisement columns on the front page, but what she was looking for was not there. A slight frown on her face, she made her way to the restaurant car.

The attendant allotted her a seat at a small table already tenanted by one person—the man with whom she had nearly collided in the corridor. In fact, the owner of the pigskin suitcase.

Elsie looked at him without appearing to do so. He

seemed very bland, very benevolent, and in some way impossible to explain, delightfully reassuring. He behaved in reserved British fashion, and it was not until the fruit was on the table that he spoke.

'They keep these places terribly hot,' he said.

'I know,' said Elsie. 'I wish one could have the window open.'

He gave a rueful smile. 'Impossible! Every person present except ourselves would protest.'

She gave an answering smile. Neither said any more.

Coffee was brought and the usual indecipherable bill. Having laid some notes upon it, Elsie suddenly took her courage in both hands.

'Excuse me,' she murmured. 'I saw your name upon your suitcase—Parker Pyne. Are you—are you, by any chance—?'

She hesitated and he came quickly to her rescue.

'I believe I am. That is'—he quoted from the advertisement which Elsie had noticed more than once in *The Times*, and for which she had searched vainly just now: '"Are you happy? If not, consult Mr Parker Pyne." Yes, I'm that one, all right.'

'I see,' said Elsie. 'How—how extraordinary!'

He shook his head. 'Not really. Extraordinary from your point of view, but not from mine.' He smiled reassuringly, then leaned forward. Most of the other diners had left the car. 'So you are unhappy?' he said.

'I—' began Elsie, and stopped.

'You would not have said "How extraordinary" otherwise,' he pointed out.

Elsie was silent for a minute. She felt strangely soothed by the mere presence of Mr Parker Pyne. 'Ye—es,' she admitted at last. 'I am—unhappy. At least, I am worried.'

He nodded sympathetically.

'You see,' she continued, 'a very curious thing has happened—and I don't know the least what to make of it.'

'Suppose you tell me about it,' suggested Mr Pyne.

Elsie thought of the advertisement. She and Edward had often commented on it and laughed. She had never thought that she ... perhaps she had better not ... if Mr Parker Pyne were a charlatan ... but he looked—nice!

Elsie made her decision. Anything to get this worry off her mind.

'I'll tell you. I'm going to Constantinople to join my husband. He does a lot of Oriental business, and this year he found it necessary to go there. He went a fortnight ago. He was to get things ready for me to join him. I've been very excited at the thought of it. You see, I've never been abroad before. We've been in England six months.'

'You and your husband are both American?'

'Yes.'

'And you have not, perhaps, been married very long?'

'We've been married a year and a half.'

'Happily?'

'Oh, yes! Edward's a perfect angel.' She hesitated. 'Not, perhaps, very much go to him. Just a little—well, I'd call it straightlaced. Lot of puritan ancestry and all that. But he's a *dear*,' she added hastily.

Mr Parker Pyne looked at her thoughtfully for a moment or two, then he said, 'Go on.'

'It was about a week after Edward had started. I was writing a letter in his study, and I noticed that the blotting paper was all new and clean, except for a few lines of writing across it. I'd just been reading a detective

103

story with a clue in the blotter and so, just for fun, I held it up to a mirror. It really *was* just fun, Mr Pyne— I mean, he's such a mild lamb one wouldn't dream of anything of that kind.'

'Yes, yes; I quite understand.'

'The thing was quite easy to read. First there was the word "wife" then "Simplon Express", and lower down, "just before Venice would be the best time",' she stopped.

'Curious,' said Mr Pyne. 'Distinctly curious. It was your husband's handwriting?'

'Oh, yes. But I've cudgelled my brains and I cannot see under what circumstances he would write a letter with just those words in it.'

'"Just before Venice would be the best time",' repeated Mr Parker Pyne. 'Distinctly curious.'

Mrs Jeffries was leaning forward looking at him with a flattering hopefulness. 'What shall I do?' she asked simply.

'I am afraid,' said Mr Parker Pyne, 'that we shall have to wait until before Venice.' He took up a folder from the table. 'Here is the schedule time of our train. It arrives at Venice at two twenty-seven tomorrow afternoon.'

They looked at each other.

'Leave it to me,' said Parker Pyne.

It was five minutes past two. The Simplon Express was eleven minutes late. It had passed Mestre about a quarter of an hour before.

Mr Parker Pyne was sitting with Mrs Jeffries in her compartment. So far the journey had been pleasant and uneventful. But now the moment had arrived when, if anything was going to happen, it presumably would happen. Mr Parker Pyne and Elsie faced each other.

Her heart was beating fast, and her eyes sought him in a kind of anguished appeal for reassurance.

'Keep perfectly calm,' he said. 'You are quite safe. I am here.'

Suddenly a scream broke out from the corridor.

'Oh, look—look! The train is on fire!'

With a bound Elsie and Mr Parker Pyne were in the corridor. An agitated woman with a Slav countenance was pointing a dramatic finger. Out of one of the front compartments smoke was pouring in a cloud. Mr Parker Pyne and Elsie ran along the corridor. Others joined them. The compartment in question was full of smoke. The first comers drew back, coughing. The conductor appeared.

'The compartment is empty!' he cried. 'Do not alarm yourselves, *messieurs et dames*. *Le feu*, it will be controlled.'

A dozen excited questions and answers broke out. The train was running over the bridge that joins Venice to the mainland.

Suddenly Mr Parker Pyne turned, forced his way through the little pack of people behind him and hurried down the corridor to Elsie's compartment. The lady with the Slav face was seated in it, drawing deep breaths from the open window.

'Excuse me, Madame,' said Parker Pyne. 'But this is not your compartment.'

'I know. I know,' said the Slav lady. '*Pardon*. It is the shock, the emotion—my heart.' She sank back on the seat and indicated the open window. She drew in her breath in great gasps.

Mr Parker Pyne stood in the doorway. His voice was fatherly and reassuring. 'You must not be afraid,' he said. 'I do not think for a moment the fire is serious.'

'Not? Ah, what a mercy! I feel restored.' She half-rose. 'I will return to my compartment.'

'Not just yet.' Mr Parker Pyne's hand pressed her gently back. 'I will ask you to wait a moment, Madame.'

'Monsieur, this is an outrage!'

'Madame, you will remain.'

His voice rang out coldly. The woman sat still looking at him. Elsie joined them.

'It seems it was a smoke bomb,' she said breathlessly. 'Some ridiculous practical joke. The conductor is furious. He is asking everybody—' She broke off, staring at the second occupant of the carriage.

'Mrs Jeffries,' said Mr Parker Pyne, 'what do you carry in your little scarlet case?'

'My jewellery.'

'Perhaps you would be so kind as to look and see that everything is there.'

There was immediately a torrent of words from the Slav lady. She broke into French, the better to do justice to her feelings.

In the meantime Elsie had picked up the jewel case. 'Oh!' she cried. 'It's unlocked.'

'*Et je porterai plainte à la Compagnie des Wagons-Lits*,' finished the Slav lady.

'They're gone!' cried Elsie. 'Everything! My diamond bracelet. And the necklace Pop gave me. And the emerald and ruby rings. And some lovely diamond brooches. Thank goodness I was wearing my pearls. Oh, Mr Pyne, what shall we do?'

'If you will fetch the conductor,' said Mr Parker Pyne, 'I will see that this woman does not leave this compartment till he comes.'

'*Scélérat! Monstre!*' shrieked the Slav lady. She went on to further insults. The train drew in to Venice.

The events of the next half-hour may be briefly summarized. Mr Parker Pyne dealt with several different officials in several different languages—and suffered defeat. The suspected lady consented to be searched—and emerged without a stain on her character. The jewels were not on her.

Between Venice and Trieste Mr Parker Pyne and Elsie discussed the case.

'When was the last time you actually saw your jewels?'

'This morning. I put away some sapphire earrings I was wearing yesterday and took out a pair of plain pearl ones.'

'And all the jewellery was there intact?'

'Well, I didn't go through it all, naturally. But it looked the same as usual. A ring or something like that might have been missing, but no more.'

Mr Parker Pyne nodded. 'Now, when the conductor made up the compartment this morning?'

'I had the case with me—in the restaurant car. I always take it with me. I've never left it except when I ran out just now.'

'Therefore,' said Mr Parker Pyne, 'that injured innocent, Madame Subayska, or whatever she calls herself, *must* have been the thief. But what the devil did she do with the things? She was only in here a minute and a half—just time to open the case with a duplicate key and take out the stuff—yes, but what next?'

'Could she have handed them to anyone else?'

'Hardly. I had turned back and was forcing my way along the corridor. If anyone had come out of this compartment I should have seen them.'

'Perhaps she threw them out of the window to someone.'

'An excellent suggestion; only, as it happens, we were

passing over the sea at that moment. We were on the bridge.'

'Then she must have hidden them actually in the carriage.'

'Let's hunt for them.'

With true transatlantic energy Elsie began to look about. Mr Parker Pyne participated in the search in a somewhat absent fashion. Reproached for not trying, he excused himself.

'I'm thinking that I must send a rather important telegram at Trieste,' he explained.

Elsie received the explanation coldly. Mr Parker Pyne had fallen heavily in her estimation.

'I'm afraid you're annoyed with me, Mrs Jeffries,' he said meekly.

'Well, you've not been very successful,' she retorted.

'But, my dear lady, you must remember I am not a detective. Theft and crime are not in my line at all. The human heart is my province.'

'Well, I was a bit unhappy when I got on this train,' said Elsie, 'but nothing to what I am now! I could just cry buckets. My lovely, lovely bracelet—and the emerald ring Edward gave me when we were engaged.'

'But surely you are insured against theft?' Mr Parker Pyne interpolated.

'Am I? I don't know. Yes, I suppose I am. But it's the *sentiment* of the thing, Mr Pyne.'

The train slackened speed. Mr Parker Pyne peered out of the window. 'Trieste,' he said. 'I must send my telegram.'

'Edward!' Elsie's face lighted up as she saw her husband hurrying to meet her on the platform at Stamboul. For the moment even the loss of her jewellery faded from her mind. She forgot the curious words she had found on the blotter. She forgot everything except that it was a fortnight since she had seen her husband last, and that in spite of being sober and straightlaced he was really a most attractive person.

They were just leaving the station when Elsie felt a friendly tap on the shoulder and turned to see Mr Parker Pyne. His bland face was beaming good-naturedly.

'Mrs Jeffries,' he said, 'will you come to see me at the Hotel Tokatlian in half an hour? I think I may have some good news for you.'

Elsie looked uncertainly at Edward. Then she made the introduction. 'This—er—is my husband—Mr Parker Pyne.'

'As I believe your wife wired you, her jewels have been stolen,' said Mr Parker Pyne. 'I have been doing what I can to help her recover them. I think I may have news for her in about half an hour.'

Elsie looked enquiringly at Edward. He replied promptly: 'You'd better go, dear. The Tokatlian, you said, Mr Pyne? Right; I'll see she makes it.'

It was just a half an hour later that Elsie was shown into Mr Parker Pyne's private sitting room. He rose to receive her.

'You've been disappointed in me, Mrs Jeffries,' he said. 'Now, don't deny it. Well, I don't pretend to be a magician but I do what I can. Take a look inside here.'

He passed along the table a small stout cardboard box. Elsie opened it. Rings, brooches, bracelets, necklace—they were all there.

'Mr Pyne, how marvellous! How—how too wonderful!'

Mr Parker Pyne smiled modestly. 'I am glad not to have failed you, my dear young lady.'

'Oh, Mr Pyne, you make me feel just mean! Ever since Trieste I've been horrid to you. And now—this. But how did you get hold of them? When? Where?'

Mr Parker Pyne shook his head thoughtfully. 'It's a long story,' he said. 'You may hear it one day. In fact, you may hear it quite soon.'

'Why can't I hear it now?'

'There are reasons,' said Mr Parker Pyne.

And Elsie had to depart with her curiosity unsatisfied.

When she had gone, Mr Parker Pyne took up his hat and stick and went out into the streets of Pera. He walked along smiling to himself, coming at last to a little café, deserted at the moment, which overlooked the Golden Horn. On the other side, the mosques of Stamboul showed slender minarets against the afternoon sky. It was very beautiful. Mr Pyne sat down and ordered two coffees. They came thick and sweet. He had just begun to sip his when a man slipped into the seat opposite. It was Edward Jeffries.

'I have ordered some coffee for you,' said Mr Parker Pyne, indicating the little cup.

Edward pushed the coffee aside. He leaned forward across the table. 'How did you know?' he asked.

Mr Parker Pyne sipped his coffee dreamily. 'Your wife will have told you about her discovery on the blotter? No? Oh, but she will tell you; it has slipped her mind for the moment.'

He mentioned Elsie's discovery.

'Very well; that linked up perfectly with the curious incident that happened just before Venice. For some reason or other you were engineering the theft of your wife's jewels. But why the phrase "just before Venice would be the best time"? There seemed nonsense in that. Why did you not leave it to your—agent—to choose her own time and place?

'And then, suddenly, I saw the point. *Your wife's jewels were stolen before you yourself left London and were replaced by paste duplicates.* But that solution did not satisfy you. You were a high-minded, conscientious young man. You have a horror of some servant or other innocent person being suspected. A theft must actually occur—at a place and in a manner which will leave no suspicion attached to anybody of your acquaintance or household.

'Your accomplice is provided with a key to the jewel box and a smoke bomb. At the correct moment she gives the alarm, darts into your wife's compartment, unlocks the jewel case and flings the paste duplicates into the sea. She may be suspected and searched, but nothing can be proved against her, since the jewels are not in her possession.

'And now the significance of the place chosen becomes apparent. If the jewels had merely been thrown out by the side of the line, they might have been found. Hence the importance of the one moment when the train is passing over the sea.

'In the meantime, you make your arrangements for selling the jewellery here. You have only to hand over the stones when the robbery has actually taken place. My wire, however, reached you in time. You obeyed my instructions and deposited the box of jewellery at the Tokatlian to await my arrival, knowing that otherwise I should keep my threat of placing the matter in the hands of the police. You also obeyed my instructions in joining me here.'

Edward Jeffries looked at Mr Parker Pyne appealingly. He was a good-looking young man, tall and fair, with a round chin and very round eyes. 'How can I make you understand?' he said hopelessly. 'To you I must seem just a common thief.'

'Not at all,' said Mr Parker Pyne. 'On the contrary, I should say you are almost painfully honest. I am accustomed to the classification of types. You, my dear sir, fall naturally into the category of victims. Now, tell me the whole story.'

'I can tell you in one word—blackmail.'

'Yes?'

'You've seen my wife: you realize what a pure, innocent creature she is—without knowledge or thought of evil.'

'Yes, yes.'

'She has the most marvellously pure ideals. If she were to find out about—about anything I had done, she would leave me.'

'I wonder. But that is not the point. What *have* you done, my young friend? I presume there is some affair with a woman?'

Edward Jeffries nodded.

'Since your marriage—or before?'

'Before—oh, before.'

'Well, well, what happened?'

'Nothing, nothing at all. This is just the cruel part of it. It was at a hotel in the West Indies. There was a very attractive woman—a Mrs Rossiter—staying there. Her husband was a violent man; he had the most savage fits of temper. One night he threatened her with a revolver. She escaped from him and came to my room. She was half-crazy with terror. She—she asked me to let her stay there till morning. I—what else could I do?'

Mr Parker Pyne gazed at the young man, and the young man gazed back with conscious rectitude. Mr

Parker Pyne sighed. 'In other words, to put it plainly, you were had for a mug, Mr Jeffries.'

'Really—'

'Yes, yes. A very old trick—but it often comes off successfully with quixotic young men. I suppose, when your approaching marriage was announced, the screw was turned?'

'Yes. I received a letter. If I did not send a certain sum of money, everything would be disclosed to my prospective father-in-law. How I had—had alienated this young woman's affection from her husband; how she had been seen coming to my room. The husband would bring a suit for divorce. Really, Mr Pyne, the whole thing made me out the most utter blackguard.'

He wiped his brow in a harassed manner.

'Yes, yes, I know. And so you paid. And from time to time the screw has been put on again.'

'Yes. This was the last straw. Our business has been badly hit by the slump. I simply could not lay my hands on any ready money. I hit upon this plan.' He picked up his cup of cold coffee, looked at it absently, and drank it. 'What am I to do now?' he demanded pathetically. 'What *am* I to do, Mr Pyne?'

'You will be guided by me,' said Parker Pyne firmly. 'I will deal with your tormentors. As to your wife, you will go straight back to her and tell her the truth—or at least a portion of it. The only point where you will deviate from the truth is concerning the actual facts in the West Indies. You must conceal from her the fact that you were—well, had for a mug, as I said before.'

'But—'

'My dear Mr Jeffries, you do not understand women. If a woman has to choose between a mug and a Don Juan, she will choose Don Juan every time. Your wife,

Mr Jeffries, is a charming, innocent, high-minded girl, and the only way she is going to get any kick out of her life with you is to believe that she has reformed a rake.'

Edward Jeffries was staring at him, open-mouthed.

'I mean what I say,' said Mr Parker Pyne. 'At the present moment your wife is in love with you, but I see signs that she may not remain so if you continue to present to her a picture of such goodness and rectitude that it is almost synonymous with dullness.'

'Go to her, my boy,' said Mr Parker Pyne kindly. 'Confess everything—that is, as many things as you can think of. Then explain that from the moment you met her you gave up all this life. You even stole so that it might not come to her ears. She will forgive you enthusiastically.'

'But when there's nothing really to forgive—'

'What is truth?' said Mr Parker Pyne. 'In my experience it is usually the thing that upsets the apple cart! It is a fundamental axiom of married life that you *must* lie to a woman. She likes it! Go and be forgiven, my boy. And live happily ever afterwards. I dare say your wife will keep a wary eye on you in future whenever a pretty woman comes along—some men would mind that, but I don't think you will.'

'I never want to look at any other woman but Elsie,' said Mr Jeffries simply.

'Splendid, my boy,' said Mr Parker Pyne. 'But I shouldn't let her know that if I were you. No woman likes to feel she's taken on too soft a job.'

Edward Jeffries rose. 'You really think—?'

'I *know*,' said Mr Parker Pyne, with force.

The Jewel Robbery at the Grand Metropolitan

'Poirot,' I said, 'a change of air would do you good.'

'You think so, *mon ami?*'

'I am sure of it.'

'Eh—eh?' said my friend, smiling. 'It is all arranged, then?'

'You will come?'

'Where do you propose to take me?'

'Brighton. As a matter of fact, a friend of mine in the City put me on to a very good thing, and—well, I have money to burn, as the saying goes. I think a weekend at the Grand Metropolitan would do us all the good in the world.'

'Thank you, I accept most gratefully. You have the good heart to think of an old man. And the good heart, it is in the end worth all the little grey cells. Yes, yes, I who speak to you am in danger of forgetting that sometimes.'

I did not relish the implication. I fancy that Poirot is sometimes a little inclined to underestimate my mental capacities. But his pleasure was so evident that I put my slight annoyance aside.

'Then, that's all right,' I said hastily.

Saturday evening saw us dining at the Grand Metropolitan in the midst of a gay throng. All the world and his wife seemed to be at Brighton. The dresses were marvellous, and the jewels—worn sometimes with

115

more love of display than good taste—were something magnificent.

'*Hein*, it is a good sight, this!' murmured Poirot. 'This is the home of the Profiteer, is it not so, Hastings?'

'Supposed to be,' I replied. 'But we'll hope they aren't all tarred with the Profiteering brush.'

Poirot gazed round him placidly.

'The sight of so many jewels makes me wish I had turned my brains to crime, instead of to its detection. What a magnificent opportunity for some thief of distinction! Regard, Hastings, that stout woman by the pillar. She is, as you would say, plastered with gems.'

I followed his eyes.

'Why,' I exclaimed, 'it's Mrs Opalsen.'

'You know her?'

'Slightly. Her husband is a rich stockbroker who made a fortune in the recent oil boom.'

After dinner we ran across the Opalsens in the lounge, and I introduced Poirot to them. We chatted for a few minutes, and ended by having our coffee together.

Poirot said a few words in praise of some of the costlier gems displayed on the lady's ample bosom, and she brightened up at once.

'It's a perfect hobby of mine, Mr Poirot. I just *love* jewellery. Ed knows my weakness, and every time things go well he brings me something new. You are interested in precious stones?'

'I have had a good deal to do with them one time and another, madame. My profession has brought me into contact with some of the most famous jewels in the world.'

He went on to narrate, with discreet pseudonyms, the story of the historic jewels of a reigning house, and Mrs Opalsen listened with bated breath.

'There now,' she exclaimed, as he ended. 'If it isn't just like a play! You know, I've got some pearls of my own that have a history attached to them. I believe it's supposed to be one of the finest necklaces in the world—the pearls are so beautifully matched and so perfect in colour. I declare I really must run up and get it!'

'Oh, madame,' protested Poirot, 'you are too amiable. Pray do not derange yourself!'

'Oh, but I'd like to show it to you.'

The buxom dame waddled across to the lift briskly enough. Her husband, who had been talking to me, looked at Poirot inquiringly.

'Madame your wife is so amiable as to insist on showing me her pearl necklace,' explained the latter.

'Oh, the pearls!' Opalsen smiled in a satisfied fashion. 'Well, they *are* worth seeing. Cost a pretty penny too! Still, the money's there all right; I could get what I paid for them any day—perhaps more. May have to, too, if things go on as they are now. Money's confoundedly tight in the City. All this infernal EPD.' He rambled on, launching into technicalities where I could not follow him.

He was interrupted by a small page-boy who approached him and murmured something in his ear.

'Eh—what? I'll come at once. Not taken ill, is she? Excuse me, gentlemen.'

He left us abruptly. Poirot leaned back and lit one of his tiny Russian cigarettes. Then, carefully and meticulously, he arranged the empty coffee-cups in a neat row, and beamed happily on the result.

The minutes passed. The Opalsens did not return.

'Curious,' I remarked, at length. 'I wonder when they will come back.'

Poirot watched the ascending spirals of smoke, and then said thoughtfully:

'They will not come back.'

'Why?'

'Because, my friend, something has happened.'

'What sort of thing? How do you know?' I asked curiously.

Poirot smiled.

'A few minutes ago the manager came hurriedly out of his office and ran upstairs. He was much agitated. The liftboy is deep in talk with one of the pages. The lift-bell has rung three times, but he heeds it not. Thirdly, even the waiters are *distrait*; and to make a waiter *distrait*—' Poirot shook his head with an air of finality. 'The affair must indeed be of the first magnitude. Ah, it is as I thought! Here come the police.'

Two men had just entered the hotel—one in uniform, the other in plain clothes. They spoke to a page, and were immediately ushered upstairs. A few minutes later, the same boy descended and came up to where we were sitting.

'Mr Opalsen's compliments, and would you step upstairs?'

Poirot sprang nimbly to his feet. One would have said that he awaited the summons. I followed with no less alacrity.

The Opalsens' apartments were situated on the first floor. After knocking on the door, the page-boy retired, and we answered the summons. 'Come in!' A strange scene met our eyes. The room was Mrs Opalsen's bedroom, and in the centre of it, lying back in an armchair, was the lady herself, weeping violently. She presented an extraordinary spectacle, with the tears making great furrows in the powder with which her complexion was liberally coated. Mr Opalsen was striding up and down angrily. The two police officials stood in the middle of the room, one with a notebook in hand. An hotel chambermaid, looking frightened to death, stood by the fireplace; and on the other side of the room a French-woman, obviously Mrs Opalsen's maid, was weeping and wringing her hands, with an intensity of grief that rivalled that of her mistress.

Into this pandemonium stepped Poirot, neat and smiling. Immediately, with an energy surprising in one of her bulk Mrs Opalsen sprang from her chair towards him.

'There now; Ed may say what he likes, but I believe in luck, I do. It was fated I should meet you the way I did this evening, and I've a feeling that if you can't get my pearls back for me nobody can.'

'Calm yourself, I pray of you, madame.' Poirot patted her hand soothingly. 'Reassure yourself. All will be well. Hercule Poirot will aid you!'

Mr Opalsen turned to the police inspector.

'There will be no objection to my—er—calling in this gentleman, I suppose?'

'None at all, sir,' replied the man civilly, but with complete indifference. 'Perhaps now your lady's feeling better she'll just let us have the facts?'

Mrs Opalsen looked helplessly at Poirot. He led her back to her chair.

'Seat yourself, madame, and recount to us the whole history without agitating yourself.'

Thus abjured, Mrs Opalsen dried her eyes gingerly, and began.

'I came upstairs after dinner to fetch my pearls for Mr Poirot here to see. The chambermaid and Célestine were both in the room as usual—'

'Excuse me, madame, but what do you mean by "as usual"?'

Mr Opalsen explained.

'I make it a rule that no one is to come into this room unless Célestine, the maid, is there also. The chambermaid does the room in the morning while Célestine is present, and comes in after dinner to turn down the beds under the same conditions; otherwise she never enters the room.'

'Well, as I was saying,' continued Mrs Opalsen, 'I came up. I went to the drawer here'—she indicated the bottom right-hand drawer of the knee-hole dressing-table—'took out my jewel-case and unlocked it. It seemed quite as usual—but the pearls were not there!'

The inspector had been busy with his notebook. 'When had you last seen them?' he asked.

'They were there when I went down to dinner.'

'You are sure?'

'Quite sure. I was uncertain whether to wear them or not, but in the end I decided on the emeralds, and put them back in the jewel-case.'

'Who locked up the jewel-case?'

'I did. I wear the key on a chain round my neck.' She held it up as she spoke.

The inspector examined it, and shrugged his shoulders.

'The thief must have had a duplicate key. No difficult matter. The lock is quite a simple one. What did you do after you'd locked the jewel-case?'

'I put it back in the bottom drawer where I always keep it.'

'You didn't lock the drawer?'

'No, I never do. My maid remains in the room till I come up, so there's no need.'

The inspector's face grew greyer.

'Am I to understand that the jewels were there when you went down to dinner, and that since then *the maid has not left the room?*'

Suddenly, as though the horror of her own situation for the first time burst upon her, Célestine uttered a piercing shriek, and, flinging herself upon Poirot, poured out a torrent of incoherent French.

The suggestion was infamous! That she should be suspected of robbing Madame! The police were well known to be of a stupidity incredible! But Monsieur, who was a Frenchman—

'A Belgian,' interjected Poirot, but Célestine paid no attention to the correction.

Monsieur would not stand by and see her falsely accused, while that infamous chambermaid was allowed to go scot-free. She had never liked her—a bold, red-faced thing—a born thief. She had said from the first that she was not honest. And had kept a sharp watch over her too, when she was doing Madame's room! Let those idiots of policemen search her, and if they did not find Madame's pearls on her it would be very surprising!

Although this harangue was uttered in rapid and virulent French, Célestine had interlarded it with a wealth of gesture, and the chambermaid realized at least a part of her meaning. She reddened angrily.

'If that foreign woman's saying I took the pearls, it's a lie!' she declared heatedly. 'I never so much as saw them.'

'Search her!' screamed the other. 'You will find it is as I say.'

'You're a liar—do you hear?' said the chambermaid, advancing upon her. 'Stole 'em yourself, and want to put it on me. Why, I was only in the room about three minutes before the lady came up, and then you were sitting here the whole time, as you always do, like a cat watching a mouse.'

The inspector looked across inquiringly at Célestine. 'Is that true? Didn't you leave the room at all?'

'I did not actually leave her alone,' admitted Célestine reluctantly, 'but I went into my own room through the door here twice—once to fetch a reel of cotton, and once for my scissors. She must have done it then.'

'You wasn't gone a minute,' retorted the chambermaid angrily. 'Just popped out and in again. I'd be glad if the police *would* search me. *I've* nothing to be afraid of.'

At this moment there was a tap at the door. The inspector went to it. His face brightened when he saw who it was.

'Ah!' he said. 'That's rather fortunate. I sent for one of our female searchers, and she's just arrived. Perhaps if you wouldn't mind going into the room next door.'

He looked at the chambermaid, who stepped across the threshold with a toss of her head, the searcher following her closely.

The French girl had sunk sobbing into a chair. Poirot was looking round the room, the main features of which I have made clear by a sketch.

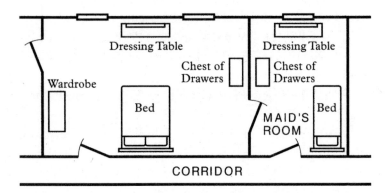

'Where does that door lead?' he inquired, nodding his head towards the one by the window.

'Into the next apartment, I believe,' said the inspector. 'It's bolted, anyway, on this side.'

Poirot walked across to it, tried it, then drew back the bolt and tried it again.

'And on the other side as well,' he remarked. 'Well, that seems to rule out that.'

He walked over to the windows, examining each of them in turn.

'And again—nothing. Not even a balcony outside.'

'Even if there were,' said the inspector impatiently, 'I don't see how that would help us, if the maid never left the room.'

'*Évidemment*,' said Poirot, not disconcerted. 'As Mademoiselle is positive she did not leave the room—'

He was interrupted by the reappearance of the chambermaid and the police searcher.

'Nothing,' said the latter laconically.

'I should hope not, indeed,' said the chambermaid virtuously. 'And that French hussy ought to be ashamed of herself taking away an honest girl's character.'

'There, there, my girl; that's all right,' said the inspector, opening the door. 'Nobody suspects you. You go along and get on with your work.'

The chambermaid went unwillingly.

'Going to search *her*?' she demanded, pointing at Célestine.

'Yes, yes!' He shut the door on her and turned the key.

Célestine accompanied the searcher into the small room in her turn. A few minutes later she also returned. Nothing had been found on her.

The inspector's face grew graver.

'I'm afraid I'll have to ask you to come along with me all the same, miss.' He turned to Mrs Opalsen. 'I'm sorry, madam, but all the evidence points that way. If she's not got them on her, they're hidden somewhere about the room.'

Célestine uttered a piercing shriek, and clung to Poirot's arm. The latter bent and whispered something in the girl's ear. She looked up at him doubtfully.

'*Si, si, mon enfant*—I assure you it is better not to resist.' Then he turned to the inspector. 'You permit, monsieur? A little experiment—purely for my own satisfaction.'

'Depends on what it is,' replied the police officer noncommittally.

Poirot addressed Célestine once more.

'You have told us that you went into your room to fetch a reel of cotton. Whereabouts was it?'

'On top of the chest of drawers, monsieur.'

'And the scissors?'

'They also.'

'Would it be troubling you too much, mademoiselle, to ask you to repeat those two actions? You were sitting here with your work, you say?'

Célestine sat down, and then, at a sign from Poirot, rose, passed into the adjoining room, took up an object from the chest of drawers, and returned.

Poirot divided his attention between her movements and a large turnip of a watch which he held in the palm of his hand.

'Again, if you please, mademoiselle.'

At the conclusion of the second performance, he made a note in his pocket-book, and returned the watch to his pocket.

'Thank you, mademoiselle. And you, monsieur'—he bowed to the inspector—'for your courtesy.'

The inspector seemed somewhat entertained by this excessive politeness. Célestine departed in a flood of tears, accompanied by the woman and the plain-clothes official.

Then, with a brief apology to Mrs Opalsen, the inspector set to work to ransack the room. He pulled out drawers, opened cupboards, completely unmade the bed, and tapped the floor. Mr Opalsen looked on sceptically.

'You really think you will find them?'

'Yes, sir. It stands to reason. She hadn't time to take them out of the room. The lady's discovering the robbery so soon upset her plans. No, they're here right enough. One of the two must have hidden them— and it's very unlikely for the chambermaid to have done so.'

'More than unlikely—impossible!' said Poirot quietly.

'Eh?' The inspector stared.

Poirot smiled modestly.

'I will demonstrate. Hastings, my good friend, take my watch in your hand—with care. It is a family heir-loom! Just now I timed Mademoiselle's movements— her first absence from the room was of twelve seconds, her second of fifteen. Now observe my actions. Madame will have the kindness to give me the key of the jewel-case. I thank you. My friend Hastings will have the kindness to say "Go!"'

'Go!' I said.

With almost incredible swiftness, Poirot wrenched open the drawer of the dressing-table, extracted the jewel-case, fitted the key in the lock, opened the case, selected a piece of jewellery, shut and locked the case, and returned it to the drawer, which he pushed to again. His movements were like lightning.

'Well, *mon ami*?' he demanded of me breathlessly.

'Forty-six seconds,' I replied.

'You see?' He looked round. 'There would have not been time for the chambermaid even to take the necklace out, far less hide it.'

'Then that settles it on the maid,' said the inspector with satisfaction, and returned to his search. He passed into the maid's bedroom next door.

Poirot was frowning thoughtfully. Suddenly he shot a question at Mr Opalsen.

'This necklace—it was, without doubt, insured?'

Mr Opalsen looked a trifle surprised at the question.

'Yes,' he said hesitatingly, 'that is so.'

'But what does that matter?' broke in Mrs Opalsen tearfully. 'It's my necklace I want. It was unique. No money could be the same.'

'I comprehend, madame,' said Poirot soothingly. 'I comprehend perfectly. To *la femme* sentiment is everything—is it not so? But, monsieur, who has not the so fine susceptibility, will doubtless find some slight consolation in the fact.'

'Of course, of course,' said Mr Opalsen rather uncertainly. 'Still—'

He was interrupted by a shout of triumph from the inspector. He came in dangling something from his fingers.

With a cry, Mrs Opalsen heaved herself up from her chair. She was a changed woman.

'Oh, oh, my necklace!'

She clasped it to her breast with both hands. We crowded round.

'Where was it?' demanded Opalsen.

'Maid's bed. In among the springs of the wire mattress. She must have stolen it and hidden it there before the chambermaid arrived on the scene.'

'You permit, madame?' said Poirot gently. He took the necklace from her and examined it closely; then handed it back with a bow.

'I'm afraid, madame, you'll have to hand it over to us for the time being,' said the inspector. 'We shall want it for the charge. But it shall be returned to you as soon as possible.'

Mr Opalsen frowned.

'Is that necessary?'

'I'm afraid so, sir. Just a formality.'

'Oh, let him take it, Ed!' cried his wife. 'I'd feel safer if he did. I shouldn't sleep a wink thinking someone else might try to get hold of it. That wretched girl! And I would never have believed it of her.'

'There, there, my dear, don't take on so.'

I felt a gentle pressure on my arm. It was Poirot.

'Shall we slip away, my friend? I think our services are no longer needed.'

Once outside, however, he hesitated, and then, much to my surprise, he remarked:

'I should rather like to see the room next door.'

The door was not locked, and we entered. The room, which was a large double one, was unoccupied. Dust lay about rather noticeably, and my sensitive friend gave a characteristic grimace as he ran his finger round a rectangular mark on a table near the window.

'The *service* leaves to be desired,' he observed dryly.

He was staring thoughtfully out of the window, and seemed to have fallen into a brown study.

'Well?' I demanded impatiently. 'What did we come in here for?'

He started.

'*Je vous demande pardon, mon ami*. I wished to see if the door was really bolted on this side also.'

'Well,' I said, glancing at the door which communicated with the room we had just left, 'it *is* bolted.'

Poirot nodded. He still seemed to be thinking.

'And anyway,' I continued, 'what does it matter? The case is over. I wish you'd had more chance of distinguishing yourself. But it was the kind of case that even a stiff-backed idiot like that inspector couldn't go wrong over.'

Poirot shook his head.

'The case is not over, my friend. It will not be over until we find out who stole the pearls.'

'But the maid did!'

'Why do you say that?'

'Why,' I stammered, 'they were found—actually in her mattress.'

'Ta, ta, ta!' said Poirot impatiently. 'Those were not the pearls.'

'What?'

'Imitation, *mon ami.*'

The statement took my breath away. Poirot was smiling placidly.

'The good inspector obviously knows nothing of jewels. But presently there will be a fine hullabaloo!'

'Come!' I cried, dragging at his arm.

'Where?'

'We must tell the Opalsens at once.'

'I think not.'

'But that poor woman—'

'*Eh bien*; that poor woman, as you call her, will have a much better night believing the jewels to be safe.'

'But the thief may escape with them!'

'As usual, my friend, you speak without reflection. How do you know that the pearls Mrs Opalsen locked up so carefully tonight were not the false ones, and that the real robbery did not take place at a much earlier date?'

'Oh!' I said, bewildered.

'Exactly,' said Poirot, beaming. 'We start again.'

He led the way out of the room, paused a moment as though considering, and then walked down to the end of the corridor, stopping outside the small den where the chambermaids and valets of the respective floors congregated. Our particular chambermaid appeared to be holding a small court there, and to be retailing her late experiences to an appreciative audience. She stopped in the middle of a sentence. Poirot bowed with his usual politeness.

'Excuse that I derange you, but I shall be obliged if you will unlock for me the door of Mr Opalsen's room.'

The woman rose willingly, and we accompanied her down the passage again. Mr Opalsen's room was on the other side of the corridor, its door facing that of his wife's room. The chambermaid unlocked it with her pass-key, and we entered.

As she was about to depart Poirot detained her.

'One moment; have you ever seen among the effects of Mr Opalsen a card like this?'

He held out a plain white card, rather highly glazed and uncommon in appearance. The maid took it and scrutinized it carefully.

'No, sir, I can't say I have. But, anyway, the valet has most to do with the gentlemen's rooms.'

'I see. Thank you.'

Poirot took back the card. The woman departed. Poirot appeared to reflect a little. Then he gave a short, sharp nod of the head.

'Ring the bell, I pray you, Hastings. Three times for the valet.'

I obeyed, devoured with curiosity. Meanwhile Poirot had emptied the waste-paper basket on the floor, and was swiftly going through its contents.

In a few moments the valet answered the bell. To him Poirot put the same question, and handed him the card to examine. But the response was the same. The valet had never seen a card of that particular quality among Mr Opalsen's belongings. Poirot thanked him, and he withdrew, somewhat unwillingly, with an inquisitive glance at the overturned waste-paper basket and the litter on the floor. He could hardly have helped over-hearing Poirot's thoughtful remark as he bundled the torn papers back again:

'And the necklace was heavily insured . . .'

'Poirot,' I cried, 'I see—'

'You see nothing, my friend,' he replied quickly. 'As usual, nothing at all! It is incredible—but there it is. Let us return to our own apartments.'

We did so in silence. Once there, to my intense surprise, Poirot effected a rapid change of clothing.

'I go to London tonight,' he explained. 'It is imperative.'

'What?'

'Absolutely. The real work, that of the brain (ah, those brave little grey cells), it is done. I go to seek the con-firmation. I shall find it! Impossible to deceive Hercule Poirot!'

'You'll come a cropper one of these days,' I observed, rather disgusted by his vanity.

'Do not be enraged, I beg of you, *mon ami*. I count on you to do me a service—of your friendship.'

'Of course,' I said eagerly, rather ashamed of my moroseness. 'What is it?'

'The sleeve of my coat that I have taken off—will you brush it? See you, a little white powder has clung to it. You without doubt observed me run my finger round the drawer of the dressing-table?'

'No, I didn't.'

'You should observe my actions, my friend. Thus I obtained the powder on my finger, and, being a little overexcited, I rubbed it on my sleeve; an action without method which I deplore—false to all my principles.'

'But what was the powder?' I asked, not particularly interested in Poirot's principles.

'Not the poison of the Borgias,' replied Poirot with a twinkle. 'I see your imagination mounting. I should say it was French chalk.'

'French chalk?'

'Yes, cabinet-makers use it to make drawers run smoothly.'

I laughed.

'You old sinner! I thought you were working up to something exciting.'

'*Au revoir*, my friend. I save myself. I fly!'

The door shut behind him. With a smile, half of derision, half of affection, I picked up the coat and stretched out my hand for the clothes brush.

The next morning, hearing nothing from Poirot, I went out for a stroll, met some old friends, and lunched with them at their hotel. In the afternoon we went for a spin. A punctured tyre delayed us, and it was past eight when I got back to the Grand Metropolitan.

The first sight that met my eyes was Poirot, looking even more diminutive than usual, sandwiched between the Opalsens, beaming in a state of placid satisfaction.

'*Mon ami* Hastings!' he cried, and sprang to meet me. 'Embrace me, my friend; all has marched to a marvel!'

Luckily, the embrace was merely figurative—not a thing one is always sure of with Poirot.

'Do you mean—' I began.

'Just wonderful, I call it!' said Mrs Opalsen, smiling all over her fat face. 'Didn't I tell you, Ed, that if he couldn't get back my pearls nobody would?'

'You did, my dear, you did. And you were right.'

I looked helplessly at Poirot, and he answered the glance.

'My friend Hastings is, as you say in England, all at the seaside. Seat yourself, and I will recount to you all the affair that has so happily ended.'

'Ended?'

'But yes. They are arrested.'

'Who are arrested?'

'The chambermaid and the valet, *parbleu*! You did not suspect? Not with my parting hint about the French chalk?'

'You said cabinet-makers used it.'

'Certainly they do—to make drawers slide easily. Somebody wanted the drawer to slide in and out without any noise. Who could that be? Obviously, only the chambermaid. The plan was so ingenious that it did not at once leap to the eye—not even to the eye of Hercule Poirot.

'Listen, this was how it was done. The valet was in the empty room next door, waiting. The French maid leaves the room. Quick as a flash the chambermaid whips open the drawer, takes out the jewel-case and, slipping back the bolt, passes it through the door. The valet opens it at his leisure with the duplicate key with which he has provided himself, extracts the necklace, and waits his time. Célestine leaves the room again, and—pst!—in a flash the case is passed back again and replaced in the drawer.

132

'Madame arrives, the theft is discovered. The chambermaid demands to be searched, with a good deal of righteous indignation, and leaves the room without a stain on her character. The imitation necklace with which they have provided themselves has been concealed in the French girl's bed that morning by the chambermaid—a master stroke, *ça*!'

'But what did you go to London for?'

'You remember the card?'

'Certainly. It puzzled me—and puzzles me still. I thought—'

I hesitated delicately, glancing at Mr Opalsen.

Poirot laughed heartily.

'*Une blague*! For the benefit of the valet. The card was one with a specially prepared surface—for fingerprints. I went straight to Scotland Yard, asked for our old friend Inspector Japp, and laid the facts before him. As I had suspected, the fingerprints proved to be those of two well-known jewel thieves who have been "wanted" for some time. Japp came down with me, the thieves were arrested, and the necklace was discovered in the valet's possession. A clever pair, but they failed in *method*. Have I not told you, Hastings, at least thirty-six times, that without method—'

'At least thirty-six thousand times!' I interrupted. 'But where did their "method" break down?'

'*Mon ami*, it is a good plan to take a place as chambermaid or valet—but you must not shirk your work. They left an empty room undusted; and therefore, when the man put down the jewel-case on the little table near the communicating door, it left a square mark—'

'I remember,' I cried.

'Before, I was undecided. Then—I *knew*!'

There was a moment's silence.

'And I've got my pearls,' said Mrs Opalsen as a sort of Greek chorus.

'Well,' I said, 'I'd better have some dinner.'

Poirot accompanied me.

'This ought to mean kudos for you,' I observed.

'*Pas du tout*,' replied Poirot tranquilly. 'Japp and the local inspector will divide the credit between them. But'—he tapped his pocket—'I have a cheque here, from Mr Opalsen, and, how you say, my friend? This week-end has not gone according to plan. Shall we return here next weekend—at my expense this time?'

Ingots of Gold

'I do not know that the story that I am going to tell you is a fair one,' said Raymond West, 'because I can't give you the solution of it. Yet the facts were so interesting and so curious that I should like to propound it to you as a problem. And perhaps between us we may arrive at some logical conclusion.

'The date of these happenings was two years ago, when I went down to spend Whitsuntide with a man called John Newman, in Cornwall.'

'Cornwall?' said Joyce Lemprière sharply.

'Yes. Why?'

'Nothing. Only it's odd. My story is about a place in Cornwall, too—a little fishing village called Rathole. Don't tell me yours is the same?'

'No. My village is called Polperran. It is situated on the west coast of Cornwall; a very wild and rocky spot. I had been introduced a few weeks previously and had found him a most interesting companion. A man of intelligence and independent means, he was possessed of a romantic imagination. As a result of his latest hobby he had taken the lease of Pol House. He was an authority on Elizabethan times, and he described to me in vivid and graphic language the rout of the Spanish Armada. So enthusiastic was he that one could almost imagine that he had been an eyewitness at the scene.

Is there anything in reincarnation? I wonder—I very much wonder.'

'You are so romantic, Raymond dear,' said Miss Marple, looking benignantly at him.

'Romantic is the last thing that I am,' said Raymond West, slightly annoyed. 'But this fellow Newman was chock-full of it, and he interested me for that reason as a curious survival of the past. It appears that a certain ship belonging to the Armada, and known to contain a vast amount of treasure in the form of gold from the Spanish Main, was wrecked off the coast of Cornwall on the famous and treacherous Serpent Rocks. For some years, so Newman told me, attempts had been made to salve the ship and recover the treasure. I believe such stories are not uncommon, though the number of mythical treasure ships is largely in excess of the genuine ones. A company had been formed, but had gone bankrupt, and Newman had been able to buy the rights of the thing—or whatever you call it—for a mere song. He waxed very enthusiastic about it all. According to him it was merely a question of the latest scientific, up-to-date machinery. The gold was there, and he had no doubt whatever that it could be recovered.

'It occurred to me as I listened to him how often things happen that way. A rich man such as Newman succeeds almost without effort, and yet in all probability the actual value in money of his find would mean little to him. I must say that his ardour infected me. I saw galleons drifting up the coast, flying before the storm, beaten and broken on the black rocks. The mere word galleon has a romantic sound. The phrase "Spanish Gold" thrills the schoolboy—and the grown-up man also. Moreover, I was working at the time upon a novel, some scenes of which were laid in the sixteenth century, and I saw the prospect of getting valuable local colour from my host.

'I set off that Friday morning from Paddington in high spirits, and looking forward to my trip. The carriage was empty except for one man, who sat facing me in the opposite corner. He was a tall, soldierly-looking man, and I could not rid myself of the impression that somewhere or other I had seen him before. I cudgelled my brains for some time in vain; but at last I had it. My travelling companion was Inspector Badgworth, and I had run across him when I was doing a series of articles on the Everson disappearance case.

'I recalled myself to his notice, and we were soon chatting pleasantly enough. When I told him I was going to Polperran he remarked that that was a rum coincidence, because he himself was also bound for that place. I did not like to seem inquisitive, so was careful not to ask him what took him there. Instead, I spoke of my own interest in the place, and mentioned the wrecked Spanish galleon. To my surprise the Inspector seemed to know all about it. "That will be the *Juan Fernandez*," he said. "Your friend won't be the first who has sunk money trying to get money out of her. It is a romantic notion."

'"And probably the whole story is a myth," I said. "No ship was ever wrecked there at all."

'"Oh, the ship was sunk there right enough," said the Inspector—"along with a good company of others. You would be surprised if you knew how many wrecks there are on that part of the coast. As a matter of fact, that is what takes me down there now. That is where the *Otranto* was wrecked six months ago."

'"I remember reading about it," I said. "No lives were lost, I think?"

'"No lives were lost," said the Inspector; "but

something else was lost. It is not generally known, but the *Otranto* was carrying bullion."

'"Yes?" I said, much interested.

'"Naturally we have had divers at work on salvage operations, but—*the gold has gone, Mr West.*"

'"Gone!" I said, staring at him. "How can it have gone?"

'"That is the question," said the Inspector. "The rocks tore a gaping hole in her strongroom. It was easy enough for the divers to get in that way, but they found the strongroom empty. The question is, was the gold stolen before the wreck or afterwards? Was it ever in the strongroom at all?"

'"It seems a curious case," I said.

'"It is a very curious case, when you consider what bullion is. Not a diamond necklace that you could put into your pocket. When you think how cumbersome it is and how bulky—well, the whole thing seems absolutely impossible. There may have been some hocus-pocus before the ship sailed; but if not, it must have been removed within the last six months—and I am going down to look into the matter."

'I found Newman waiting to meet me at the station. He apologized for the absence of his car, which had gone to Truro for some necessary repairs. Instead, he met me with a farm lorry belonging to the property.

'I swung myself up beside him, and we wound carefully in and out of the narrow streets of the fishing village. We went up a steep ascent, with a gradient, I should say, of one in five, ran a little distance along a winding lane, and turned in at the granite-pillared gates of Pol House.

'The place was a charming one; it was situated high up the cliffs, with a good view out to sea. Part of it was some three or four hundred years old, and a modern wing had been added. Behind it farming land of about seven or eight acres ran inland.

'"Welcome to Pol House," said Newman. "And to the Sign of the Golden Galleon." And he pointed to where, over the front door, hung a perfect reproduction of a Spanish galleon with all sails set.

'My first evening was a most charming and instructive one. My host showed me the old manuscripts relating to the *Juan Fernandez*. He unrolled charts for me and indicated positions on them with dotted lines, and he produced plans of diving apparatus, which, I may say, mystified me utterly and completely.

'I told him of my meeting with Inspector Badgworth, in which he was much interested.

'"They are a queer people round this coast," he said reflectively. "Smuggling and wrecking is in their blood. When a ship goes down on their coast they cannot help regarding it as lawful plunder meant for their pockets. There is a fellow here I should like you to see. He is an interesting survival."

'Next day dawned bright and clear. I was taken down into Polperran and there introduced to Newman's diver, a man called Higgins. He was a wooden-faced individual, extremely taciturn, and his contributions to the conversation were mostly monosyllables. After a discussion between them on highly technical matters, we adjourned to the Three Anchors. A tankard of beer somewhat loosened the worthy fellow's tongue.

'"Detective gentleman from London has come down," he grunted. "They do say that that ship that went down there last November was carrying a mortal lot of gold. Well, she wasn't the first to go down, and she won't be the last."

139

'"Hear, hear," chimed in the landlord of the Three Anchors. "That is a true word you say there, Bill Higgins."

'"I reckon it is, Mr Kelvin," said Higgins.

'I looked with some curiosity at the landlord. He was a remarkable-looking man, dark and swarthy, with curiously broad shoulders. His eyes were bloodshot, and he had a curiously furtive way of avoiding one's glance. I suspected that this was the man of whom Newman had spoken, saying he was an interesting survival.

'"We don't want interfering foreigners on this coast," he said, somewhat truculently.

'"Meaning the police?" asked Newman, smiling.

'"Meaning the police—*and others*," said Kelvin significantly. "And don't you forget it, mister."

'"Do you know, Newman, that sounded to me very like a threat," I said as we climbed the hill homewards.

'My friend laughed.

'"Nonsense; I don't do the folk down here any harm."

'I shook my head doubtfully. There was something sinister and uncivilized about Kelvin. I felt that his mind might run in strange, unrecognized channels.

'I think I date the beginning of my uneasiness from that moment. I had slept well enough that first night, but the next night my sleep was troubled and broken. Sunday dawned, dark and sullen, with an overcast sky and the threatenings of thunder in the air. I am always a bad hand at hiding my feelings, and Newman noticed the change in me.

'"What is the matter with you, West? You are a bundle of nerves this morning."

'"I don't know," I confessed, "but I have got a horrible feeling of foreboding."

'"It's the weather."

'"Yes, perhaps."

'I said no more. In the afternoon we went out in Newman's motor boat, but the rain came on with such vigour that we were glad to return to shore and change into dry clothing.

'And that evening my uneasiness increased. Outside the storm howled and roared. Towards ten o'clock the tempest calmed down. Newman looked out of the window.

'"It is clearing," he said. "I shouldn't wonder if it was a perfectly fine night in another half-hour. If so, I shall go out for a stroll."

'I yawned. "I am frightfully sleepy," I said. "I didn't get much sleep last night. I think that tonight I shall turn in early."

'This I did. On the previous night I had slept little. Tonight I slept heavily. Yet my slumbers were not restful. I was still oppressed with an awful foreboding of evil. I had terrible dreams. I dreamt of dreadful abysses and vast chasms, amongst which I was wandering, knowing that a slip of the foot meant death. I waked to find the hands of my clock pointing to eight o'clock. My head was aching badly, and the terror of my night's dreams was still upon me.

'So strongly was this so that when I went to the window and drew it up I started back with a fresh feeling of terror, for the first thing I saw, or thought I saw— was a man digging an open grave.

'It took me a minute or two to pull myself together; then I realized that the grave-digger was Newman's gardener, and the "grave" was destined to accommodate three new rose trees which were lying on the turf waiting for the moment they should be securely planted in the earth.

141

'The gardener looked up and saw me and touched his hat.

'"Good morning, sir. Nice morning, sir."

'"I suppose it is," I said doubtfully, still unable to shake off completely the depression of my spirits.

'However, as the gardener had said, it was certainly a nice morning. The sun was shining and the sky a clear pale blue that promised fine weather for the day. I went down to breakfast whistling a tune. Newman had no maids living in the house. Two middle-aged sisters, who lived in a farm-house near by, came daily to attend to his simple wants. One of them was placing the coffee-pot on the table as I entered the room.

'"Good morning, Elizabeth," I said. "Mr Newman not down yet?"

'"He must have been out very early, sir," she replied. "He wasn't in the house when we arrived."

'Instantly my uneasiness returned. On the two previous mornings Newman had come down to breakfast somewhat late; and I didn't fancy that at any time he was an early riser. Moved by those forebodings, I ran up to his bedroom. It was empty, and, moreover, his bed had not been slept in. A brief examination of his room showed me two other things. If Newman had gone out for a stroll he must have gone out in his evening clothes, for they were missing.

'I was sure now that my premonition of evil was justified. Newman had gone, as he had said he would do, for an evening stroll. For some reason or other he had not returned. Why? Had he met with an accident? Fallen over the cliffs? A search must be made at once.

'In a few hours I had collected a large band of helpers, and together we hunted in every direction along the cliffs and on the rocks below. But there was no sign of Newman.

'In the end, in despair, I sought out Inspector Badgworth. His face grew very grave.

'"It looks to me as if there has been foul play," he said. "There are some not over-scrupulous customers in these parts. Have you seen Kelvin, the landlord of the Three Anchors?"

'I said that I had seen him.

'"Did you know he did a turn in gaol four years ago? Assault and battery."

'"It doesn't surprise me," I said.

'"The general opinion in this place seems to be that your friend is a bit too fond of nosing his way into things that do not concern him. I hope he has come to no serious harm."

'The search was continued with redoubled vigour. It was not until late that afternoon that our efforts were rewarded. We discovered Newman in a deep ditch in a corner of his own property. His hands and feet were securely fastened with rope, and a handkerchief had been thrust into his mouth and secured there so as to prevent him crying out.

'He was terribly exhausted and in great pain; but after some frictioning of his wrists and ankles, and a long draught from a whisky flask, he was able to give his account of what had occurred.

'The weather having cleared, he had gone out for a stroll about eleven o'clock. His way had taken him some distance along the cliffs to a spot commonly known as Smugglers' Cove, owing to the large number of caves to be found there. Here he had noticed some men landing something from a small boat, and had strolled down to see what was going on. Whatever the stuff was it seemed to be a great weight, and it was being carried into one of the farthermost caves.

'With no real suspicion of anything being amiss, nevertheless Newman had wondered. He had drawn quite near them without being observed. Suddenly there was a cry of alarm, and immediately two powerful seafaring men had set upon him and rendered him unconscious. When next he came to himself he found himself lying on a motor vehicle of some kind, which was proceeding, with many bumps and bangs, as far as he could guess, up the lane which led from the coast to the village. To his great surprise, the lorry turned in at the gate of his own house. There, after a whispered conversation between the men, they at length drew him forth and flung him into a ditch at a spot where the depth of it rendered discovery unlikely for some time. Then the lorry drove on, and, he thought, passed out through another gate some quarter of a mile nearer the village. He could give no description of his assailants except that they were certainly seafaring men and, by their speech, Cornishmen.

'Inspector Badgworth was very interested.

'"Depend upon it that is where the stuff has been hidden," he cried. "Somehow or other it has been salvaged from the wreck and has been stored in some lonely cave somewhere. It is known that we have searched all the caves in Smugglers' Cove, and that we are now going farther afield, and they have evidently been moving the stuff at night to a cave that has been already searched and is not likely to be searched again. Unfortunately they have had at least eighteen hours to dispose of the stuff. If they got Mr Newman last night I doubt if we will find any of it there by now."

'The Inspector hurried off to make a search. He found

definite evidence that the bullion had been stored as supposed, but the gold had been once more removed, and there was no clue as to its fresh hiding-place.

'One clue there was, however, and the Inspector himself pointed it out to me the following morning.

'"That lane is very little used by motor vehicles," he said, "and in one or two places we get the traces of the tyres very clearly. There is a three-cornered piece out of one tyre, leaving a mark which is quite unmistakable. It shows going into the gate; here and there is a faint mark of it going out of the other gate, so there is not much doubt that it is the right vehicle we are after. Now, why did they take it out through the farther gate? It seems quite clear to me that the lorry came from the village. Now, there aren't many people who own a lorry in the village—not more than two or three at most. Kelvin, the landlord of the Three Anchors, has one."

'"What was Kelvin's original profession?" asked Newman.

'"It is curious that you should ask me that, Mr Newman. In his young days Kelvin was a professional diver."

'Newman and I looked at each other. The puzzle seemed to be fitting itself together piece by piece.

'"You didn't recognize Kelvin as one of the men on the beach?" asked the Inspector.

'Newman shook his head.

'"I am afraid I can't say anything as to that," he said regretfully. "I really hadn't time to see anything."

'The Inspector very kindly allowed me to accompany him to the Three Anchors. The garage was up a side street. The big doors were closed, but by going up a little alley at the side we found a small door that led into it, and the door was open. A very brief examination of the tyres sufficed for the Inspector. "We have got him, by Jove!" he exclaimed. "Here is the mark as large as life on the rear left wheel. Now, Mr Kelvin, I don't think you will be clever enough to wriggle out of this."'

Raymond West came to a halt.

'Well?' said Joyce. 'So far I don't see anything to make a problem about—unless they never found the gold.'

'They never found the gold certainly,' said Raymond. 'And they never got Kelvin either. I expect he was too clever for them, but I don't quite see how he worked it. He was duly arrested—on the evidence of the tyre mark. But an extraordinary hitch arose. Just opposite the big doors of the garage was a cottage rented for the summer by a lady artist.'

'Oh, these lady artists!' said Joyce, laughing.

'As you say, "Oh, these lady artists!" This particular one had been ill for some weeks, and, in consequence, had two hospital nurses attending her. The nurse who was on night duty had pulled her armchair up to the window, where the blind was up. She declared that the motor lorry could not have left the garage opposite without her seeing it, and she swore that in actual fact it never left the garage that night.'

'I don't think that is much of a problem,' said Joyce. 'The nurse went to sleep, of course. They always do.'

'That has—er—been known to happen,' said Mr Petherick, judiciously; 'but it seems to me that we are accepting facts without sufficient examination. Before accepting the testimony of the hospital nurse, we should inquire very closely into her bona fides. The alibi coming with such suspicious promptness is inclined to raise doubts in one's mind.'

'There is also the lady artist's testimony,' said Raymond. 'She declared that she was in pain, and awake most of the night, and that she would certainly have heard the lorry, it being an unusual noise, and the night being very quiet after the storm.'

'H'm,' said the clergyman, 'that is certainly an additional fact. Had Kelvin himself any alibi?'

'He declared that he was at home and in bed from ten o'clock onwards, but he could produce no witnesses in support of that statement.'

'The nurse went to sleep,' said Joyce, 'and so did the patient. Ill people always think they have never slept a wink all night.'

Raymond West looked inquiringly at Dr Pender.

'Do you know, I feel very sorry for that man Kelvin. It seems to me very much a case of "Give a dog a bad name." Kelvin had been in prison. Apart from the tyre mark, which certainly seems too remarkable to be coincidence, there doesn't seem to be much against him except his unfortunate record.'

'You, Sir Henry?'

Sir Henry shook his head.

'As it happens,' he said, smiling, 'I know something about this case. So clearly I mustn't speak.'

'Well, go on, Aunt Jane; haven't you got anything to say?'

'In a minute, dear,' said Miss Marple. 'I am afraid I have counted wrong. Two purl, three plain, slip one, two purl—yes, that's right. What did you say, dear?'

'What is your opinion?'

'You wouldn't like my opinion, dear. Young people never do, I notice. It is better to say nothing.'

'Nonsense, Aunt Jane; out with it.'

'Well, dear Raymond,' said Miss Marple, laying down her knitting and looking across at her nephew. 'I do think you should be more careful how you choose your friends. You are so credulous, dear, so easily gulled. I suppose it is being a writer and having so much imagination. All that story about a Spanish galleon! If you were older and had more experience of life you would have been on your guard at once. A man you had known only a few weeks, too!'

Sir Henry suddenly gave vent to a great roar of laughter and slapped his knee.

'Got you this time, Raymond,' he said. 'Miss Marple, you are wonderful. Your friend Newman, my boy, has another name—several other names in fact. At the present moment he is not in Cornwall but in Devonshire—Dartmoor, to be exact—a convict in Princetown prison. We didn't catch him over the stolen bullion business, but over the rifling of the strongroom of one of the London banks. Then we looked up his past record and we found a good portion of the gold stolen buried in the garden at Pol House. It was rather a neat idea. All along that Cornish coast there are stories of wrecked galleons full of gold. It accounted for the diver and it would account later for the gold. But a scapegoat was needed, and Kelvin was ideal for the purpose. Newman played his little comedy very well, and our friend Raymond, with his celebrity as a writer, made an unimpeachable witness.'

'But the tyre mark?' objected Joyce.

'Oh, I saw that at once, dear, although I know nothing about motors,' said Miss Marple. 'People change a wheel, you know—I have often seen them doing it—and, of course, they could take a wheel off Kelvin's lorry and take it out through the small door into the alley and put it on to Mr Newman's lorry and take the lorry out of one gate down to the beach, fill it up with the gold and bring it up through the other gate, and then they must have taken the wheel back and put it back on Mr Kelvin's lorry while, I suppose, someone else was tying up Mr Newman in a ditch. Very uncomfortable for him and probably longer before he was found than he expected. I suppose the man who called himself the gardener attended to that side of the business.'

'Why do you say, "called himself the gardener," Aunt Jane?' asked Raymond curiously.

'Well, he can't have been a real gardener, can he?' said Miss Marple. 'Gardeners don't work on Whit Monday. Everybody knows that.'

She smiled and folded up her knitting.

'It was really that little fact that put me on the right scent,' she said. She looked across at Raymond.

'When you are a householder, dear, and have a garden of your own, you will know these little things.'

The Soul of the Croupier

Mr Satterthwaite was enjoying the sunshine on the terrace at Monte Carlo.

Every year regularly on the second Sunday in January, Mr Satterthwaite left England for the Riviera. He was far more punctual than any swallow. In the month of April he returned to England, May and June he spent in London, and had never been known to miss Ascot. He left town after the Eton and Harrow match, paying a few country house visits before repairing to Deauville or Le Touquet. Shooting parties occupied most of September and October, and he usually spent a couple of months in town to wind up the year. He knew everybody and it may safely be said that everybody knew him.

This morning he was frowning. The blue of the sea was admirable, the gardens were, as always, a delight, but the people disappointed him—he thought them an ill-dressed, shoddy crowd. Some, of course, were gamblers, doomed souls who could not keep away. Those Mr Satterthwaite tolerated. They were a necessary background. But he missed the usual leaven of the *élite*—his own people.

'It's the exchange,' said Mr Satterthwaite gloomily. 'All sorts of people come here now who could never have afforded it before. And then, of course, I'm getting old ... All the young people—the people coming on—they go to these Swiss places.'

But there were others that he missed, the well-dressed Barons and Counts of foreign diplomacy, the Grand Dukes and the Royal Princes. The only Royal Prince he had seen so far was working a lift in one of the less well-known hotels. He missed, too, the beautiful and expensive ladies. There was still a few of them, but not nearly as many as there used to be.

Mr Satterthwaite was an earnest student of the drama called Life, but he liked his material to be highly coloured. He felt discouragement sweep over him. Values were changing—and he—was too old to change.

It was at that moment that he observed the Countess Czarnova coming towards him.

Mr Satterthwaite had seen the Countess at Monte Carlo for many seasons now. The first time he had seen her she had been in the company of a Grand Duke. On the next occasion she was with an Austrian Baron. In successive years her friends had been of Hebraic extraction, sallow men with hooked noses, wearing rather flamboyant jewellery. For the last year or two she was much seen with very young men, almost boys.

She was walking with a very young man now. Mr Satterthwaite happened to know him, and he was sorry. Franklin Rudge was a young American, a typical product of one of the Middle West States, eager to register impression, crude, but loveable, a curious mixture of native shrewdness and idealism. He was in Monte Carlo with a party of other young Americans of both sexes, all much of the same type. It was their first glimpse of the Old World and they were outspoken in criticism and in appreciation.

On the whole they disliked the English people in the

hotel, and the English people disliked them. Mr Satterthwaite, who prided himself on being a cosmopolitan, rather liked them. Their directness and vigour appealed to him, though their occasional solecisms made him shudder.

It occurred to him that the Countess Czarnova was a most unsuitable friend for young Franklin Rudge.

He took off his hat politely as they came abreast of him, and the Countess gave him a charming bow and smile.

She was a very tall woman, superbly made. Her hair was black, so were her eyes, and her eyelashes and eyebrows were more superbly black than any Nature had ever fashioned.

Mr Satterthwaite, who knew far more of feminine secrets than it is good for any man to know, rendered immediate homage to the art with which she was made up. Her complexion appeared to be flawless, of a uniform creamy white.

The very faint bistre shadows under her eyes were most effective. Her mouth was neither crimson nor scarlet, but a subdued wine colour. She was dressed in a very daring creation of black and white and carried a parasol of the shade of pinky red which is most helpful to the complexion.

Franklin Rudge was looking happy and important.

'There goes a young fool,' said Mr Satterthwaite to himself. 'But I suppose it's no business of mine and anyway he wouldn't listen to me. Well, well, I've bought experience myself in my time.'

But he still felt rather worried, because there was a very attractive little American girl in the party, and he was sure that she would not like Franklin Rudge's friendship with the Countess at all.

He was just about to retrace his steps in the opposite direction when he caught sight of the girl in question coming up one of the paths towards him. She wore a well-cut tailor-made 'suit' with a white muslin shirt waist, she had on good, sensible walking shoes, and carried a guide-book. There are some Americans who pass through Paris and emerge clothed as the Queen of Sheba, but Elizabeth Martin was not one of them. She was 'doing Europe' in a stern, conscientious spirit. She had high ideas of culture and art and she was anxious to get as much as possible for her limited store of money.

It is doubtful if Mr Satterthwaite thought of her as either cultured or artistic. To him she merely appeared very young.

'Good morning, Mr Satterthwaite,' said Elizabeth. 'Have you seen Franklin—Mr Rudge—anywhere about?'

'I saw him just a few minutes ago.'

'With his friend the Countess, I suppose,' said the girl sharply.

'Er—with the Countess, yes,' admitted Mr Satterthwaite.

'That Countess of his doesn't cut any ice with me,' said the girl in a rather high, shrill voice. 'Franklin's just crazy about her. *Why* I can't think.'

'She's got a very charming manner, I believe,' said Mr Satterthwaite cautiously.

'Do you know her?'

'Slightly.'

'I'm right down worried about Franklin,' said Miss Martin. 'That boy's got a lot of sense as a rule. You'd never think he'd fall for this sort of siren stuff. And he won't hear a thing, he gets madder than a hornet if anyone tries to say a word to him. Tell me, anyway—is she a real Countess?'

'I shouldn't like to say,' said Mr Satterthwaite. 'She may be.'

'That's the real Ha Ha English manner,' said Elizabeth with signs of displeasure. 'All I can say is that in Sargon Springs—that's our home town, Mr Satterthwaite— that Countess would look a mighty queer bird.'

Mr Satterthwaite thought it possible. He forebore to point out that they were not in Sargon Springs but in the principality of Monaco, where the Countess happened to synchronize with her environment a great deal better than Miss Martin did.

He made no answer and Elizabeth went on towards the Casino. Mr Satterthwaite sat on a seat in the sun, and was presently joined by Franklin Rudge.

Rudge was full of enthusiasm.

'I'm enjoying myself,' he announced with naïve enthusiasm. 'Yes, *sir*! This is what I call seeing life— rather a different kind of life from what we have in the States.'

The elder man turned a thoughtful face to him.

'Life is lived very much the same everywhere,' he said rather wearily. 'It wears different clothes—that's all.'

Franklin Rudge stared.

'I don't get you.'

'No,' said Mr Satterthwaite. 'That's because you've got a long way to travel yet. But I apologize. No elderly man should permit himself to get into the habit of preaching.'

'Oh! that's all right.' Rudge laughed, displaying the beautiful teeth of all his countrymen. 'I don't say, mind you, that I'm not disappointed in the Casino. I thought the gambling would be different—something much more feverish. It seems just rather dull and sordid to me.'

'Gambling is life and death to the gambler, but it has no great spectacular value,' said Mr Satterthwaite. 'It is more exciting to read about than to see.'

The young man nodded his agreement.

'You're by way of being rather a big bug socially, aren't you?' he asked with a diffident candour that made it impossible to take offence. 'I mean, you know all the Duchesses and Earls and Countesses and things.'

'A good many of them,' said Mr Satterthwaite. 'And also the Jews and the Portuguese and the Greeks and the Argentines.'

'Eh?' said Mr Rudge.

'I was just explaining,' said Mr Satterthwaite, 'that I move in English society.'

Franklin Rudge meditated for a moment or two.

'You know the Countess Czarnova, don't you?' he said at length.

'Slightly,' said Mr Satterthwaite, making the same answer he had made to Elizabeth.

'Now there's a woman whom it's been very interesting to meet. One's inclined to think that the aristocracy of Europe is played out and effete. That may be true of the men, but the women are different. Isn't it a pleasure to meet an exquisite creature like the Countess? Witty, charming, intelligent, generations of civilization behind her, an aristocrat to her finger-tips!'

'Is she?' asked Mr Satterthwaite.

'Well, isn't she? You know what her family are?'

'No,' said Mr Satterthwaite. 'I'm afraid I know very little about her.'

'She was a Radzynski,' explained Franklin Rudge. 'One of the oldest families in Hungary. She's had the most extraordinary life. You know that great rope of pearls she wears?'

Mr Satterthwaite nodded.

'That was given her by the King of Bosnia. She smuggled some secret papers out of the kingdom for him.'

'I heard,' said Mr Satterthwaite, 'that the pearls had been given her by the King of Bosnia.'

The fact was indeed a matter of common gossip, it being reported that the lady had been a *chère amie* of His Majesty's in days gone by.

'Now I'll tell you something more.'

Mr Satterthwaite listened, and the more he listened the more he admired the fertile imagination of the Countess Czarnova. No vulgar 'siren stuff' (as Elizabeth Martin had put it) for her. The young man was shrewd enough in that way, clean living and idealistic. No, the Countess moved austerely through a labyrinth of diplomatic intrigues. She had enemies, detractors—naturally! It was a glimpse, so the young American was made to feel, into the life of the old regime with the Countess as the central figure, aloof, aristocratic, the friend of counsellors and princes, a figure to inspire romantic devotion.

'And she's had any amount to contend against,' ended the young man warmly. 'It's an extraordinary thing but she's never found a woman who would be a real friend to her. Women have been against her all her life.'

'Probably,' said Mr Satterthwaite.

'Don't you call it a scandalous thing?' demanded Rudge hotly.

'N—no,' said Mr Satterthwaite thoughtfully. 'I don't know that I do. Women have got their own standards, you know. It's no good our mixing ourselves up in their affairs. They must run their own show.'

'I don't agree with you,' said Rudge earnestly. 'It's one of the worst things in the world today, the unkindness of woman to woman. You know Elizabeth Martin? Now she agrees with me in theory absolutely. We've often discussed it together. She's only a kid, but her ideas are all right. But the moment it comes to a practical test— why, she's as bad as any of them. Got a real down on the Countess without knowing a darned thing about her, and won't listen when I try to tell her things. It's all wrong, Mr Satterthwaite. I believe in democracy— and—what's that but brotherhood between men and sisterhood between women?'

He paused earnestly. Mr Satterthwaite tried to think of any circumstances in which a sisterly feeling might arise between the Countess and Elizabeth Martin and failed.

'Now the Countess, on the other hand,' went on Rudge, 'admires Elizabeth immensely, and thinks her charming in every way. Now what does that show?'

'It shows,' said Mr Satterthwaite dryly, 'that the Countess has lived a considerable time longer than Miss Martin has.'

Franklin Rudge went off unexpectedly at a tangent.

'Do you know how old she is? She told me. Rather sporting of her. I should have guessed her to be twenty-nine, but she told me of her own accord that she was thirty-five. She doesn't look it, does she?' Mr Satterthwaite, whose private estimate of the lady's age was between forty-five and forty-nine, merely raised his eyebrows.

'I should caution you against believing all you are told at Monte Carlo,' he murmured.

He had enough experience to know the futility of arguing with the lad. Franklin Rudge was at a pitch of white hot chivalry when he would have disbelieved any statement that was not backed with authoritative proof.

'Here is the Countess,' said the boy, rising.

She came up to them with the languid grace that so became her. Presently they all three sat down together. She was very charming to Mr Satterthwaite, but in rather an aloof manner. She deferred to him prettily, asking his opinion, and treating him as an authority on the Riviera.

The whole thing was cleverly managed. Very few minutes had elapsed before Franklin Rudge found himself gracefully but unmistakably dismissed, and the Countess and Mr Satterthwaite were left *tête-à-tête*.

She put down her parasol and began drawing patterns with it in the dust.

'You are interested in the nice American boy, Mr Satterthwaite, are you not?'

Her voice was low with a caressing note in it.

'He's a nice young fellow,' said Mr Satterthwaite, noncommittally.

'I find him sympathetic, yes,' said the Countess reflectively. 'I have told him much of my life.'

'Indeed,' said Mr Satterthwaite.

'Details such as I have told to few others,' she continued dreamily. 'I have had an extraordinary life, Mr Satterthwaite. Few would credit the amazing things that have happened to me.'

Mr Satterthwaite was shrewd enough to penetrate her meaning. After all, the stories that she had told to Franklin Rudge *might* be the truth. It was extremely unlikely, and in the last degree improbable, but it was *possible* ... No one could definitely say: 'That is not so—'

He did not reply, and the Countess continued to look out dreamily across the bay.

And suddenly Mr Satterthwaite had a strange and new impression of her. He saw her no longer as a harpy,

158

but as a desperate creature at bay, fighting tooth and nail. He stole a sideways glance at her. The parasol was down, he could see the little haggard lines at the corners of her eyes. In one temple a pulse was beating.

It flowed through him again and again—that increasing certitude. She was a creature desperate and driven. She would be merciless to him or to anyone who stood between her and Franklin Rudge. But he still felt he hadn't got the hang of the situation. Clearly she had plenty of money. She was always beautifully dressed, and her jewels were marvellous. There could be no real urgency of that kind. Was it love? Women of her age did, he well knew, fall in love with boys. It might be that. There was, he felt sure, something out of the common about the situation.

Her *tête-à-tête* with him was, he recognized, a throwing down of the gauntlet. She had singled him out as her chief enemy. He felt sure that she hoped to goad him into speaking slightingly of her to Franklin Rudge. Mr Satterthwaite smiled to himself. He was too old a bird for that. He knew when it was wise to hold one's tongue.

He watched her that night in the Cercle Privé, as she tried her fortunes at roulette.

Again and again she staked, only to see her stake swept away. She bore her losses well, with the stoical *sang froid* of the old *habitué*. She staked *en plein* once or twice, put the maximum on red, won a little on the middle dozen and then lost it again, finally she backed *manque* six times and lost every time. Then with a little graceful shrug of the shoulders she turned away.

She was looking unusually striking in a dress of gold tissue with an underlying note of green. The famous Bosnian pearls were looped round her neck and long pearl ear-rings hung from her ears.

Mr Satterthwaite heard two men near him appraise her.

'The Czarnova,' said one, 'she wears well, does she not? The Crown jewels of Bosnia look fine on her.'

The other, a small Jewish-looking man, stared curiously after her.

'So those are the pearls of Bosnia, are they?' he asked. '*En vérité*. That is odd.'

He chuckled softly to himself.

Mr Satterthwaite missed hearing more, for at the moment he turned his head and was overjoyed to recognize an old friend.

'My dear Mr Quin.' He shook him warmly by the hand. 'The last place I should ever have dreamed of seeing you.'

Mr Quin smiled, his dark attractive face lighting up.

'It should not surprise you,' he said. 'It is Carnival time. I am often here in Carnival time.'

'Really? Well, this is a great pleasure. Are you anxious to remain in the rooms? I find them rather warm.'

'It will be pleasanter outside,' agreed the other. 'We will walk in the gardens.'

The air outside was sharp, but not chill. Both men drew deep breaths.

'That is better,' said Mr Satterthwaite.

'Much better,' agreed Mr Quin. 'And we can talk freely. I am sure that there is much that you want to tell me.'

'There is indeed.'

Speaking eagerly, Mr Satterthwaite unfolded his perplexities. As usual he took pride in his power of conveying atmosphere. The Countess, young Franklin, uncompromising Elizabeth—he sketched them all in with a deft touch.

'You have changed since I first knew you,' said Mr Quin, smiling, when the recital was over.

'In what way?'

'You were content then to look on at the drama that life offered. Now—you want to take part—to act.'

'It is true,' confessed Mr Satterthwaite. 'But in this case I do not know what to do. It is all very perplexing. Perhaps—' He hesitated. 'Perhaps you will help me?'

'With pleasure,' said Mr Quin. 'We will see what we can do.'

Mr Satterthwaite had an odd sense of comfort and reliance.

The following day he introduced Franklin Rudge and Elizabeth Martin to his friend Mr Harley Quin. He was pleased to see that they got on together. The Countess was not mentioned, but at lunch time he heard news that aroused his attention.

'Mirabelle is arriving in Monte this evening,' he confided excitedly to Mr Quin.

'The Parisian stage favourite?'

'Yes. I daresay you know—it's common property— she is the King of Bosnia's latest craze. He has showered jewels on her, I believe. They say she is the most exacting and extravagant woman in Paris.'

'It should be interesting to see her and the Countess Czarnova meet tonight.'

'Exactly what I thought.'

Mirabelle was a tall, thin creature with a wonderful head of dyed fair hair. Her complexion was a pale mauve with orange lips. She was amazingly chic. She was dressed in something that looked like a glorified bird of paradise, and she wore chains of jewels hanging down her bare back. A heavy bracelet set with immense diamonds clasped her left ankle.

She created a sensation when she appeared in the Casino.

'Your friend the Countess will have a difficulty in outdoing this,' murmured Mr Quin in Mr Satterthwaite's ear.

The latter nodded. He was curious to see how the Countess comported herself.

She came late, and a low murmur ran round as she walked unconcernedly to one of the centre roulette tables.

She was dressed in white—a mere straight slip of marocain such as a débutante might have worn and her gleaming white neck and arms were unadorned. She wore not a single jewel.

'It is clever, that,' said Mr Satterthwaite with instant approval. 'She disdains rivalry and turns the tables on her adversary.'

He himself walked over and stood by the table. From time to time he amused himself by placing a stake. Sometimes he won, more often he lost.

There was a terrific run on the last dozen. The numbers 31 and 34 turned up again and again. Stakes flocked to the bottom of the cloth.

With a smile Mr Satterthwaite made his last stake for the evening, and placed the maximum on Number 5.

The Countess in her turn leant forward and placed the maximum on Number 6.

'*Faites vos jeux*,' called the croupier hoarsely. '*Rien ne va plus. Plus rien.*'

The ball span, humming merrily. Mr Satterthwaite thought to himself: '*This means something different to each of us. Agonies of hope and despair, boredom, idle amusement, life and death.*' Click!

The croupier bent forward to see.

'*Numéro cinque, rouge, impair et manque.*'

Mr Satterthwaite had won!

The croupier, having raked in the other stakes, pushed forward Mr Satterthwaite's winnings. He put out his hand to take them. The Countess did the same. The croupier looked from one to the other of them.

'*A madame,*' he said brusquely.

The Countess picked up the money. Mr Satterthwaite drew back. He remained a gentleman. The Countess looked him full in the face and he returned her glance. One or two of the people round pointed out to the croupier that he had made a mistake, but the man shook his head impatiently. He had decided. That was the end. He raised his raucous cry:

'*Faites vos jeux, Messieurs et Mesdames.*'

Mr Satterthwaite rejoined Mr Quin. Beneath his impeccable demeanour, he was feeling extremely indignant. Mr Quin listened sympathetically.

'Too bad,' he said, 'but these things happen.'

'We are to meet your friend Franklin Rudge later. I am giving a little supper party.'

The three met at midnight, and Mr Quin explained his plan.

'It is what is called a "Hedges and Highways" party,' he explained. 'We choose our meeting place, then each one goes out and is bound in honour to invite the first person he meets.'

Franklin Rudge was amused by the idea.

'Say, what happens if they won't accept?'

'You must use your utmost powers of persuasion.'

'Good. And where's the meeting place?'

'A somewhat Bohemian café—where one can take strange guests. It is called Le Caveau.'

He explained its whereabouts, and the three parted.

Mr Satterthwaite was so fortunate as to run straight into Elizabeth Martin and he claimed her joyfully. They reached Le Caveau and descended into a kind of cellar where they found a table spread for supper and lit by old-fashioned candles in candlesticks.

'We are the first,' said Mr Satterthwaite. 'Ah! here comes Franklin—'

He stopped abruptly. With Franklin was the Countess. It was an awkward moment. Elizabeth displayed less graciousness than she might have done. The Countess, as a woman of the world, retained the honours.

Last of all came Mr Quin. With him was a small, dark man, neatly dressed, whose face seemed familiar to Mr Satterthwaite. A moment later he recognized him. It was the croupier who earlier in the evening had made such a lamentable mistake.

'Let me introduce you to the company, M. Pierre Vaucher,' said Mr Quin.

The little man seemed confused. Mr Quin performed the necessary introductions easily and lightly. Supper was brought—an excellent supper. Wine came—very excellent wine. Some of the frigidity went out of the atmosphere. The Countess was very silent, so was Elizabeth. Franklin Rudge became talkative. He told various stories—not humorous stories, but serious ones. And quietly and assiduously Mr Quin passed round the wine.

'I'll tell you—and this is a true story—about a man who made good,' said Franklin Rudge impressively.

For one coming from a Prohibition country he had shown no lack of appreciation of champagne.

He told his story—perhaps at somewhat unnecessary length. It was, like many true stories, greatly inferior to fiction.

As he uttered the last word, Pierre Vaucher, opposite

him, seemed to wake up. He also had done justice to the champagne. He leaned forward across the table.

'I, too, will tell you a story,' he said thickly. 'But mine is the story of a man who did not make good. It is the story of a man who went, not up, but down the hill. And, like yours, it is a true story.'

'Pray tell it to us, monsieur,' said Mr Satterthwaite courteously.

Pierre Vaucher leant back in his chair and looked at the ceiling.

'It is in Paris that the story begins. There was a man there, a working jeweller. He was young and light-hearted and industrious in his profession. They said there was a future before him. A good marriage was already arranged for him, the bride not too bad-looking, the dowry most satisfactory. And then, what do you think? One morning he sees a girl. Such a miserable little wisp of a girl, messieurs. Beautiful? Yes, perhaps, if she were not half starved. But anyway, for this young man, she has a magic that he cannot resist. She has been struggling to find work, she is virtuous—or at least that is what she tells him. I do not know if it is true.'

The Countess's voice came suddenly out of the semi-darkness.

'Why should it not be true? There are many like that.'

'Well, as I say, the young man believed her. And he married her—an act of folly! His family would have no more to say to him. He had outraged their feelings. He married—I will call her Jeanne—it was a good action. He told her so. He felt that she should be very grateful to him. He had sacrificed much for her sake.'

'A charming beginning for the poor girl,' observed the Countess sarcastically.

'He loved her, yes, but from the beginning she

165

maddened him. She had moods—tantrums—she would be cold to him one day, passionate the next. At last he saw the truth. She had never loved him. She had married him so as to keep body and soul together. That truth hurt him, it hurt him horribly, but he tried his utmost to let nothing appear on the surface. And he still felt he deserved gratitude and obedience to his wishes. They quarrelled. She reproached him—Mon Dieu, what did she not reproach him with?

'You can see the next step, can you not? The thing that was bound to come. She left him. For two years he was alone, working in his little shop with no news of her. He had one friend—absinthe. The business did not prosper so well.

'And then one day he came into the shop to find her sitting there. She was beautifully dressed. She had rings on her hands. He stood considering her. His heart was beating—but beating! He was at a loss what to do. He would have liked to have beaten her, to have clasped her in his arms, to have thrown her down on the floor and trampled on her, to have thrown himself at her feet. He did none of those things. He took up his pincers and went on with his work. "Madame desires?" he asked formally.

'That upset her. She did not look for that, you see. "Pierre," she said, "I have come back." He laid aside his pincers and looked at her. "You wish to be forgiven?" he said. "You want me to take you back? You are sincerely repentant?" "Do you want me back?" she murmured. Oh! very softly she said it.

'He knew she was laying a trap for him. He longed to seize her in his arms, but he was too clever for that. He pretended indifference.

' "I am a Christian man," he said. "I try to do what

166

the Church directs." "Ah!" he thought, "I will humble her, humble her to her knees."

'But Jeanne, that is what I will call her, flung back her head and laughed. Evil laughter it was. "I mock myself at you, little Pierre," she said. "Look at these rich clothes, these rings and bracelets. I came to show myself to you. I thought I would make you take me in your arms and when you did so, then—*then* I would spit in your face and tell you how I hated you!"

'And on that she went out of the shop. Can you believe, messieurs, that a woman could be as evil as all that—to come back only to torment me?'

'No,' said the Countess. 'I would not believe it, and any man who was not a fool would not believe it either. But all men are blind fools.'

Pierre Vaucher took no notice of her. He went on.

'And so that young man of whom I tell you sank lower and lower. He drank more absinthe. The little shop was sold over his head. He became of the dregs, of the gutter. Then came the war. Ah! it was good, the war. It took that man out of the gutter and taught him to be a brute beast no longer. It drilled him—and sobered him. He endured cold and pain and the fear of death—but he did not die and when the war ended, he was a man again.

'It was then, messieurs, that he came South. His lungs had been affected by the gas, they said he must find work in the South. I will not weary you with all the things he did. Suffice it to say that he ended up as a croupier, and there—there in the Casino one evening, he saw her again—the woman who had ruined his life. She did not recognize him, but he recognized her. She appeared to be rich and to lack for nothing—but messieurs, the eyes of a croupier are sharp. There came

167

an evening when she placed her last stake in the world on the table. Ask me not how I know—I do know—one feels these things. Others might not believe. She still had rich clothes—why not pawn them, one would say? But to do that—pah! your credit is gone at once. Her jewels? Ah no! Was I not a jeweller in my time? Long ago the real jewels have gone. The pearls of a King are sold one by one, are replaced with false. And meantime one must eat and pay one's hotel bill. Yes, and the rich men—well, they have seen one about for many years. Bah! they say—she is over fifty. A younger chicken for my money.'

A long shuddering sigh came out of the windows where the Countess leant back.

'Yes. It was a great moment, that. Two nights I have watched her. Lose, lose, and lose again. And now the end. She put all on one number. Beside her, an English milord stakes the maximum also—on the next number. The ball rolls . . . The moment has come, she has lost . . .

'Her eyes meet mine. What do I do? I jeopardize my place in the Casino. I rob the English milord. "*A Madame*" I say, and pay over the money.'

'Ah!' There was a crash, as the Countess sprang to her feet and leant across the table, sweeping her glass on to the floor.

'Why?' she cried. 'That's what I want to know, *why* did you do it?'

There was a long pause, a pause that seemed interminable, and still those two facing each other across the table looked and looked . . . It was like a duel.

A mean little smile crept across Pierre Vaucher's face. He raised his hands.

'Madame,' he said, 'there is such a thing as pity . . .'
'Ah!'

She sank down again.

'I see.'

She was calm, smiling, herself again.

'An interesting story, M. Vaucher, is it not? Permit me to give you a light for your cigarette.'

She deftly rolled up a spill, and lighted it at the candle and held it towards him. He leaned forward till the flame caught the tip of the cigarette he held between his lips.

Then she rose unexpectedly to her feet.

'And now I must leave you all. Please—I need no one to escort me.'

Before one could realize it she was gone. Mr Satterthwaite would have hurried out after her, but he was arrested by a startled oath from the Frenchman.

'A thousand thunders!'

He was staring at the half-burned spill which the Countess had dropped on the table. He unrolled it.

'Mon Dieu!' he muttered. 'A fifty thousand franc bank note. You understand? Her winnings tonight. All that she had in the world. And she lighted my cigarette with it! Because she was too proud to accept—pity. Ah! proud, she was always proud as the Devil. She is unique—wonderful.'

He sprang up from his seat and darted out. Mr Satterthwaite and Mr Quin had also risen. The waiter approached Franklin Rudge.

'La note, monsieur,' he observed unemotionally.

Mr Quin rescued it from him quickly.

'I feel kind of lonesome, Elizabeth,' remarked Franklin Rudge. 'These foreigners—they beat the band! I don't understand them. What's it all mean, anyhow?'

He looked across at her.

'Gee, it's good to look at anything so hundred per

cent American as you.' His voice took on the plaintive note of a small child. 'These foreigners are so *odd*.'

They thanked Mr Quin and went out into the night together. Mr Quin picked up his change and smiled across at Mr Satterthwaite, who was preening himself like a contented bird.

'Well,' said the latter. 'That's all gone off splendidly. Our pair of love birds will be all right now.'

'Which ones?' asked Mr Quin.

'Oh!' said Mr Satterthwaite, taken aback. 'Oh! yes, well, I suppose you are right, allowing for the Latin point of view and all that—'

He looked dubious.

Mr Quin smiled, and a stained glass panel behind him invested him for just a moment in a motley garment of coloured light.

The Girl in the Train

'And that's that!' observed George Rowland ruefully, as he gazed up at the imposing smoke-grimed façade of the building he had just quitted.

It might be said to represent very aptly the power of Money—and Money, in the person of William Rowland, uncle to the aforementioned George, had just spoken its mind very freely. In the course of a brief ten minutes, from being the apple of his uncle's eye, the heir to his wealth, and a young man with a promising business career in front of him, George had suddenly become one of the vast army of the unemployed.

'And in these clothes they won't even give me the dole,' reflected Mr Rowland gloomily, 'and as for writing poems and selling them at the door at twopence (or "what you care to give, lydy") I simply haven't got the brains.'

It was true that George embodied a veritable triumph of the tailor's art. He was exquisitely and beautifully arrayed. Solomon and the lilies of the field were simply not in it with George. But man cannot live by clothes alone—unless he has had some considerable training in the art—and Mr Rowland was painfully aware of the fact.

'And all because of that rotten show last night,' he reflected sadly.

The rotten show last night had been a Covent Garden Ball. Mr Rowland had returned from it at a somewhat late—or rather early—hour—as a matter of fact, he could not strictly say that he remembered returning at all. Rogers, his uncle's butler, was a helpful fellow, and could doubtless give more details on the matter. A splitting head, a cup of strong tea, and an arrival at the office at five minutes to twelve instead of half-past nine had precipitated the catastrophe. Mr Rowland, senior, who for twenty-four years had condoned and paid up as a tactful relative should, had suddenly abandoned these tactics and revealed himself in a totally new light. The inconsequence of George's replies (the young man's head was still opening and shutting like some mediaeval instrument of the Inquisition) had displeased him still further. William Rowland was nothing if not thorough. He cast his nephew adrift upon the world in a few short succinct words, and then settled down to his interrupted survey of some oilfields in Peru.

George Rowland shook the dust of his uncle's office from off his feet, and stepped out into the City of London. George was a practical fellow. A good lunch, he considered, was essential to a review of the situation. He had it. Then he retraced his steps to the family mansion. Rogers opened the door. His well-trained face expressed no surprise at seeing George at this unusual hour.

'Good afternoon, Rogers. Just pack up my things for me, will you? I'm leaving here.'

'Yes, sir. Just for a short visit, sir?'

'For good, Rogers. I am going to the colonies this afternoon.'

'Indeed, sir?'

'Yes. That is, if there is a suitable boat. Do you know anything about the boats, Rogers?'

'Which colony were you thinking of visiting, sir?'

'I'm not particular. Any of 'em will do. Let's say Australia. What do you think of the idea, Rogers?'

Rogers coughed discreetly.

'Well, sir, I've certainly heard it said that there's room out there for anyone who really wants to work.'

Mr Rowland gazed at him with interest and admiration.

'Very neatly put, Rogers. Just what I was thinking myself. I shan't go to Australia—not today, at any rate. Fetch me an *A.B.C.*, will you? We will select something nearer at hand.'

Rogers brought the required volume. George opened it at random and turned the pages with a rapid hand.

'Perth—too far away—Putney Bridge—too near at hand. Ramsgate? I think not. Reigate also leaves me cold. Why—what an extraordinary thing! There's actually a place called Rowland's Castle. Ever heard of it, Rogers?'

'I fancy, sir, that you go there from Waterloo.'

'What an extraordinary fellow you are, Rogers. You know everything. Well, well, Rowland's Castle! I wonder what sort of a place it is.'

'Not much of a place, I should say, sir.'

'All the better; there'll be less competition. These quiet little country hamlets have a lot of the old feudal spirit knocking about. The last of the original Rowlands ought to meet with instant appreciation. I shouldn't wonder if they elected me mayor in a week.'

He shut up the *A.B.C.* with a bang.

'The die is cast. Pack me a small suit-case, will you, Rogers? Also my compliments to the cook, and will she oblige me with the loan of the cat. Dick Whittington, you know. When you set out to become a Lord Mayor, a cat is essential.'

'I'm sorry, sir, but the cat is not available at the present moment.'

'How is that?'

'A family of eight, sir. Arrived this morning.'

'You don't say so. I thought its name was Peter.'

'So it is, sir. A great surprise to all of us.'

'A case of careless christening and the deceitful sex, eh? Well, well, I shall have to go catless. Pack up those things at once, will you?'

'Very good, sir.'

Rogers hesitated, then advanced a little farther into the room.

'You'll excuse the liberty, sir, but if I was you, I shouldn't take too much notice of anything Mr Rowland said this morning. He was at one of those city dinners last night, and—'

'Say no more,' said George. 'I understand.'

'And being inclined to gout—'

'I know, I know. Rather a strenuous evening for you, Rogers, with two of us, eh? But I've set my heart on distinguishing myself at Rowland's Castle—the cradle of my historic race—that would go well in a speech, wouldn't it? A wire to me there, or a discreet advertisement in the morning papers, will recall me at any time if a fricassée of veal is in preparation. And now—to Waterloo!—as Wellington said on the eve of the historic battle.'

Waterloo Station was not at its brightest and best that afternoon. Mr Rowland eventually discovered a train that would take him to his destination, but it was an undistinguished train, an unimposing train—a train that nobody seemed anxious to travel by. Mr Rowland had a first-class carriage to himself, up in the front of the train. A fog was descending in an indeterminate way over the metropolis, now it lifted, now it descended. The platform was deserted, and only the asthmatic breathing of the engine broke the silence.

And then, all of a sudden, things began to happen with bewildering rapidity.

A girl happened first. She wrenched open the door and jumped in, rousing Mr Rowland from something perilously near a nap, exclaiming as she did so: 'Oh! hide me—oh! please hide me.'

George was essentially a man of action—his not to reason why, his but to do and die, etc. There is only one place to hide in a railway carriage—under the seat. In seven seconds the girl was bestowed there, and George's suit-case, negligently standing on end, covered her retreat. None too soon. An infuriated face appeared at the carriage window.

'My niece! You have her here. I want my niece.'

George, a little breathless, was reclining in the corner, deep in the sporting column of the evening paper, one-thirty edition. He laid it aside with the air of a man recalling himself from far away.

'I beg your pardon, sir?' he said politely.

'My niece—what have you done with her?'

Acting on the policy that attack is always better than defence, George leaped into action.

'What the devil do you mean?' he cried, with a very creditable imitation of his own uncle's manner.

The other paused a minute, taken aback by this sudden fierceness. He was a fat man, still panting a little as though he had run some way. His hair was cut *en brosse*, and he had a moustache of the Hohenzollern persuasion. His accents were decidedly guttural, and the stiffness of his carriage denoted that he was more at home in uniform than out of it. George had the true-born Briton's prejudice against foreigners—and an especial distaste for German-looking foreigners.

'What the devil do you mean, sir?' he repeated angrily.

'She came in here,' said the other. 'I saw her. What have you done with her?'

George flung aside the paper and thrust his head and shoulders through the window.

'So that's it, is it?' he roared. 'Blackmail. But you've tried it on the wrong person. I read all about you in the *Daily Mail* this morning. Here, guard, guard!'

Already attracted from afar by the altercation, that functionary came hurrying up.

'Here, guard,' said Mr Rowland, with that air of authority which the lower classes so adore. 'This fellow is annoying me. I'll give him in charge for attempted blackmail if necessary. Pretends I've got his niece hidden in here. There's a regular gang of these foreigners trying this sort of thing on. It ought to be stopped. Take him away, will you? Here's my card if you want it.'

The guard looked from one to the other. His mind was soon made up. His training led him to despise foreigners, and to respect and admire well-dressed gentlemen who travelled first class.

He laid his hand on the shoulder of the intruder.

'Here,' he said, 'you come out of this.'

At this crisis the stranger's English failed him, and he plunged into passionate profanity in his native tongue.

'That's enough of that,' said the guard. 'Stand away, will you? She's due out.'

Flags were waved and whistles were blown. With an unwilling jerk the train drew out of the station.

George remained at his observation post until they were clear of the platform. Then he drew in his head, and picking up the suit-case tossed it into the rack.

'It's quite all right. You can come out,' he said reassuringly.

The girl crawled out.

'Oh!' she gasped. 'How can I thank you?'

'That's quite all right. It's been a pleasure, I assure you,' returned George nonchalantly.

He smiled at her reassuringly. There was a slightly puzzled look in her eyes. She seemed to be missing something to which she was accustomed. At that moment, she caught sight of herself in the narrow glass opposite, and gave a heartfelt gasp.

Whether the carriage cleaners do, or do not, sweep under the seats every day is doubtful. Appearances were against their doing so, but it may be that every particle of dirt and smoke finds its way there like a homing bird. George had hardly had time to take in the girl's appearance, so sudden had been her arrival, and so brief the space of time before she crawled into hiding, but it was certainly a trim and well-dressed young woman who had disappeared under the seat. Now her little red hat was crushed and dented, and her face was disfigured with long streaks of dirt.

'Oh!' said the girl.

She fumbled for her bag. George, with the tact of a true gentleman, looked fixedly out of the window and admired the streets of London south of the Thames.

'How can I thank you?' said the girl again.

Taking this as a hint that conversation might now be resumed, George withdrew his gaze, and made another polite disclaimer, but this time with a good deal of added warmth in his manner.

The girl was absolutely lovely! Never before, George told himself, had he seen such a lovely girl. The *empressement* of his manner became even more marked.

'I think it was simply splendid of you,' said the girl with enthusiasm.

'Not at all. Easiest thing in the world. Only too pleased been of use,' mumbled George.

'Splendid,' she reiterated emphatically.

It is undoubtedly pleasant to have the loveliest girl you have even seen gazing into your eyes and telling you how splendid you are. George enjoyed it as much as anyone could.

Then there came a rather difficult silence. It seemed to dawn upon the girl that further explanation might be expected. She flushed a little.

'The awkward part of it is,' she said nervously, 'that I'm afraid I can't explain.'

She looked at him with a piteous air of uncertainty.

'You can't explain?'

'No.'

'How perfectly splendid!' said Mr Rowland with enthusiasm.

'I beg your pardon?'

'I said, how perfectly splendid. Just like one of those books that keep you up all night. The heroine always says "I can't explain" in the first chapter. She explains in the last, of course, and there's never any real reason why she shouldn't have done so in the beginning— except that it would spoil the story. I can't tell you how pleased I am to be mixed up in a real mystery— I didn't know there were such things. I hope it's got something to do with secret documents of immense importance, and the Balkan express. I dote upon the Balkan express.'

The girl stared at him with wide, suspicious eyes.

'What makes you say the Balkan express?' she asked sharply.

'I hope I haven't been indiscreet,' George hastened to put in. 'Your uncle travelled by it, perhaps.'

'My uncle—' She paused, then began again. 'My uncle—'

'Quite so,' said George sympathetically. 'I've got an uncle myself. Nobody should be held responsible for their uncles. Nature's little throwbacks—that's how I look at it.'

The girl began to laugh suddenly. When she spoke George was aware of the slight foreign inflection in her voice. At first he had taken her to be English.

'What a refreshing and unusual person you are, Mr—'

'Rowland. George to my friends.'

'My name is Elizabeth—'

She stopped abruptly.

'I like the name of Elizabeth,' said George, to cover her momentary confusion. 'They don't call you Bessie, or anything horrible like that, I hope?'

She shook her head.

'Well,' said George, 'now that we know each other, we'd better get down to business. If you'll stand up, Elizabeth, I'll brush down the back of your coat.'

She stood up obediently, and George was as good as his word.

'Thank you, Mr Rowland.'

'George. George to my friends, remember. And you can't come into my nice empty carriage, roll under the seat, induce me to tell lies to your uncle, and then refuse to be friends, can you?'

'Thank you, George.'

'That's better.'

'Do I look quite all right now?' asked Elizabeth, trying to see over her left shoulder.

'You look—oh! you look—you look all right,' said George, curbing himself sternly.

'It was all so sudden, you see,' explained the girl.

'It must have been.'

'He saw us in the taxi, and then at the station I just bolted in here knowing he was close behind me. Where is this train going to, by the way?'

'Rowland's Castle,' said George firmly.

The girl looked puzzled.

'Rowland's Castle?'

'Not at once, of course. Only after a good deal of stopping and slow going. But I confidently expect to be there before midnight. The old South-Western was a very reliable line—slow but sure—and I'm sure the Southern Railway is keeping up the old traditions.'

'I don't know that I want to go to Rowland's Castle,' said Elizabeth doubtfully.

'You hurt me. It's a delightful spot.'

'Have you ever been there?'

'Not exactly. But there are lots of other places you can go to, if you don't fancy Rowland's Castle. There's Woking, and Weybridge, and Wimbledon. The train is sure to stop at one or other of them.'

'I see,' said the girl. 'Yes, I can get out there, and perhaps motor back to London. That would be the best plan, I think.'

Even as she spoke, the train began to slow up. Mr Rowland gazed at her with appealing eyes.

'If I can do anything—'

'No, indeed. You've done a lot already.'

There was a pause, then the girl broke out suddenly:

'I—I wish I could explain. I—'

'For heaven's sake don't do that! It would spoil everything. But look here, isn't there anything that I could do? Carry the secret papers to Vienna—or something of that kind? There always are secret papers. Do give me a chance.'

The train had stopped. Elizabeth jumped quickly out on to the platform. She turned and spoke to him through the window.

'Are you in earnest? Would you really do something for us—for me?'

'I'd do anything in the world for you, Elizabeth.'

'Even if I could give you no reasons?'

'Rotten things, reasons!'

'Even if it were—dangerous?'

'The more danger, the better.'

She hesitated a minute then seemed to make up her mind.

'Lean out of the window. Look down the platform as though you weren't really looking.' Mr Rowland endeavoured to comply with this somewhat difficult recommendation. 'Do you see that man getting in— with a small dark beard—light overcoat? Follow him, see what he does and where he goes.'

'Is that all?' asked Mr Rowland. 'What do I—?'

She interrupted him.

'Further instructions will be sent to you. Watch him—and guard this.' She thrust a small sealed packet into his hand. 'Guard it with your life. It's the key to everything.'

The train went on. Mr Rowland remained staring out of the window, watching Elizabeth's tall, graceful figure threading its way down the platform. In his hand he clutched the small sealed packet.

The rest of his journey was both monotonous and uneventful. The train was a slow one. It stopped everywhere. At every station, George's head shot out of the window, in case his quarry should alight. Occasionally he strolled up and down the platform when the wait promised to be a long one, and reassured himself that the man was still there.

The eventual destination of the train was Portsmouth, and it was there that the black-bearded traveller alighted. He made his way to a small second-class hotel where he booked a room. Mr Rowland also booked a room.

The rooms were in the same corridor, two doors from each other. The arrangement seemed satisfactory to George. He was a complete novice in the art of shadowing, but was anxious to acquit himself well, and justify Elizabeth's trust in him.

At dinner George was given a table not far from that of his quarry. The room was not full, and the majority of the diners George put down as commercial travellers, quiet respectable men who ate their food with appetite. Only one man attracted his special notice, a small man with ginger hair and moustache and a suggestion of horsiness in his apparel. He seemed to be interested in George also, and suggested a drink and a game of billiards when the meal had come to a close. But George had just espied the black-bearded man putting on his hat and overcoat, and declined politely. In another minute he was out in the street, gaining fresh insight into the difficult art of shadowing. The chase was a long and a weary one—and in the end it seemed to lead nowhere. After twisting and turning through the streets of Portsmouth for about four miles, the man returned to the hotel, George hard upon his heels. A faint doubt assailed the latter. Was it possible that the man was aware of his presence? As he debated this point, standing in the hall, the outer door was pushed open, and the little ginger man entered. Evidently he, too, had been out for a stroll.

George was suddenly aware that the beauteous damsel in the office was addressing him.

'Mr Rowland, isn't it? Two gentlemen have called to see you. Two foreign gentlemen. They are in the little room at the end of the passage.'

Somewhat astonished, George sought the room in question. Two men who were sitting there, rose to their feet and bowed punctiliously.

'Mr Rowland? I have no doubt, sir, that you can guess our identity.'

George gazed from one to the other of them. The spokesman was the elder of the two, a grey-haired, pompous gentleman who spoke excellent English. The other was a tall, somewhat pimply young man, with a blond Teutonic cast of countenance which was not rendered more attractive by the fierce scowl which he wore at the present moment.

Somewhat relieved to find that neither of his visitors was the old gentleman he had encountered at Waterloo, George assumed his most debonair manner.

'Pray sit down, gentlemen. I'm delighted to make your acquaintance. How about a drink?'

The elder man held up a protesting hand.

'Thank you, Lord Rowland—not for us. We have but a few brief moments—just time for you to answer a question.'

'It's very kind of you to elect me to the peerage,' said George. 'I'm sorry you won't have a drink. And what is this momentous question?'

'Lord Rowland, you left London in company with a certain lady. You arrived here alone. Where is the lady?'

George rose to his feet.

'I fail to understand the question,' he said coldly, speaking as much like the hero of a novel as he could.

'I have the honour to wish you good-evening, gentle-men.'

'But you do understand it. You understand it per-fectly,' cried the younger man, breaking out suddenly. 'What have you done with Alexa?'

'Be calm, sir,' murmured the other. 'I beg of you to be calm.'

'I can assure you,' said George, 'that I know no lady of that name. There is some mistake.'

The older man was eyeing him keenly.

'That can hardly be,' he said drily. 'I took the liberty of examining the hotel register. You entered yourself as Mr G Rowland of Rowland's Castle.'

George was forced to blush.

'A—a little joke of mine,' he explained feebly.

'A somewhat poor subterfuge. Come, let us not beat about the bush. Where is Her Highness?'

'If you mean Elizabeth—'

With a howl of rage the young man flung himself forward again.

'Insolent pig-dog! To speak of her thus.'

'I am referring,' said the other slowly, 'as you very well know, to the Grand Duchess Anastasia Sophia Alexandra Marie Helena Olga Elizabeth of Catonia.'

'Oh!' said Mr Rowland helplessly.

He tried to recall all that he had ever known of Catonia. It was, as far as he remembered, a small Balkan kingdom, and he seemed to remember something about a revolution having occurred there. He rallied himself with an effort.

'Evidently we mean the same person,' he said cheer-fully, 'only *I* call her Elizabeth.'

'You will give me satisfaction for that,' snarled the younger man. 'We will fight.'

184

'Fight?'

'A duel.'

'I never fight duels,' said Mr Rowland firmly.

'Why not?' demanded the other unpleasantly.

'I'm too afraid of getting hurt.'

'Aha! is that so? Then I will at least pull your nose for you.'

The younger man advanced fiercely. Exactly what happened was difficult to see, but he described a sudden semi-circle in the air and fell to the ground with a heavy thud. He picked himself up in a dazed manner. Mr Rowland was smiling pleasantly.

'As I was saying,' he remarked, 'I'm always afraid of getting hurt. That's why I thought it well to learn jujitsu.'

There was a pause. The two foreigners looked doubt-fully at this amiable looking young man, as though they suddenly realized that some dangerous quality lurked behind the pleasant nonchalance of his manner. The younger Teuton was white with passion.

'You will repent this,' he hissed.

The older man retained his dignity.

'That is your last word, Lord Rowland? You refuse to tell us Her Highness's whereabouts?'

'I am unaware of them myself.'

'You can hardly expect me to believe that.'

'I am afraid you are of an unbelieving nature, sir.'

The other merely shook his head, and murmuring: 'This is not the end. You will hear from us again,' the two men took their leave.

George passed his hand over his brow. Events were proceeding at a bewildering rate. He was evidently mixed up in a first-class European scandal.

'It might even mean another war,' said George

hopefully, as he hunted round to see what had become of the man with the black beard.

To his great relief, he discovered him sitting in a corner of the commercial-room. George sat down in another corner. In about three minutes the black-bearded man got up and went up to bed. George followed and saw him go into his room and close the door. George heaved a sigh of relief.

'I need a night's rest,' he murmured. 'Need it badly.'

Then a dire thought struck him. Supposing the black-bearded man had realized that George was on his trail? Supposing that he should slip away during the night whilst George himself was sleeping the sleep of the just? A few minutes' reflection suggested to Mr Rowland a way of dealing with his difficulty. He unravelled one of his socks till he got a good length of neutral-coloured wool, then creeping quietly out of his room, he pasted one end of the wool to the farther side of the stranger's door with stamp paper, carrying the wool across it and along to his own room. There he hung the end with a small silver bell—a relic of last night's entertainment. He surveyed these arrangements with a good deal of satisfaction. Should the black-bearded man attempt to leave his room George would be instantly warned by the ringing of the bell.

This matter disposed of, George lost no time in seeking his couch. The small packet he placed carefully under his pillow. As he did so, he fell into a momentary brown study. His thoughts could have been translated thus:

'Anastasia Sophia Marie Alexandra Olga Elizabeth. Hang it all, I've missed out one. I wonder now—'

He was unable to go to sleep immediately, being tantalized with his failure to grasp the situation. What was it all about? What was the connection between the escaping Grand Duchess, the sealed packet and the black-bearded man? What was the Grand Duchess escaping from? Were the foreigners aware that the sealed packet was in his possession? What was it likely to contain?

Pondering these matters, with an irritated sense that he was no nearer the solution, Mr Rowland fell asleep.

He was awakened by the faint jangle of a bell. Not one of those men who awake to instant action, it took him just a minute and a half to realize the situation. Then he jumped up, thrust on some slippers, and, opening the door with the utmost caution, slipped out into the corridor. A faint moving patch of shadow at the far end of the passage showed him the direction taken by his quarry. Moving as noiselessly as possible, Mr Rowland followed the trail. He was just in time to see the black-bearded man disappear into a bathroom. That was puzzling, particularly so as there was a bathroom just opposite his own room. Moving up close to the door, which was ajar, George peered through the crack. The man was on his knees by the side of the bath, doing something to the skirting board immediately behind it. He remained there for about five minutes, then he rose to his feet, and George beat a prudent retreat. Safe in the shadow of his own door, he watched the other pass and regain his own room.

'Good,' said George to himself. 'The mystery of the bathroom will be investigated tomorrow morning.'

He got into bed and slipped his hand under the pillow to assure himself that the precious packet was still there. In another minute, he was scattering the bedclothes in a panic. The packet was gone!

It was a sadly chastened George who sat consuming eggs and bacon the following morning. He had failed

Elizabeth. He had allowed the precious packet she had entrusted to his charge to be taken from him, and the 'Mystery of the Bathroom' was miserably inadequate. Yes, undoubtedly George had made a mutt of himself.

After breakfast he strolled upstairs again. A chambermaid was standing in the passage looking perplexed.

'Anything wrong, my dear?' said George kindly.

'It's the gentleman here, sir. He asked to be called at half-past eight, and I can't get any answer and the door's locked.'

'You don't say so,' said George.

An uneasy feeling rose in his own breast. He hurried into his room. Whatever plans he was forming were instantly brushed aside by a most unexpected sight. There on the dressing-table was the little packet which had been stolen from him the night before!

George picked it up and examined it. Yes, it was undoubtedly the same. But the seals had been broken. After a minute's hesitation, he unwrapped it. If other people had seen its contents there was no reason why he should not see them also. Besides, it was possible that the contents had been abstracted. The unwound paper revealed a small cardboard box, such as jewellers use. George opened it. Inside, nestling on a bed of cotton wool, was a plain gold wedding ring.

He picked it up and examined it. There was no inscription inside— nothing whatever to make it out from any other wedding ring. George dropped his head into his hands with a groan.

'Lunacy,' he murmured. 'That's what it is. Stark staring lunacy. There's no sense anywhere.'

Suddenly he remembered the chambermaid's statement, and at the same time he observed that there was a broad parapet outside the window. It was not a feat he would ordinarily have attempted, but he was so aflame with curiosity and anger that he was in the mood to make light of difficulties. He sprang upon the window sill. A few seconds later he was peering in at the window of the room occupied by the black-bearded man. The window was open and the room was empty. A little further along was a fire escape. It was clear how the quarry had taken his departure.

George jumped in through the window. The missing man's effects were still scattered about. There might be some clue amongst them to shed light on George's perplexities. He began to hunt about, starting with the contents of a battered kit-bag.

It was a sound that arrested his search—a very slight sound, but a sound indubitably in the room. George's glance leapt to the big wardrobe. He sprang up and wrenched open the door. As he did so, a man jumped out from it and went rolling over the floor locked in George's embrace. He was no mean antagonist. All George's special tricks availed very little. They fell apart at length in sheer exhaustion, and for the first time George saw who his adversary was It was the little man with the ginger moustache.

'Who the devil are you?' demanded George.

For answer the other drew out a card and handed it to him. George read it aloud.

'Detective-Inspector Jarrold, Scotland Yard.'

'That's right, sir. And you'd do well to tell me all you know about this business.'

'I would, would I?' said George thoughtfully. 'Do you know, Inspector, I believe you're right. Shall we adjourn to a more cheerful spot?'

In a quiet corner of the bar George unfolded his soul. Inspector Jarrold listened sympathetically.

'Very puzzling, as you say, sir,' he remarked when George had finished. 'There's a lot as I can't make head or tail of myself, but there's one or two points I can clear up for you. I was here after Mardenberg (your black-bearded friend) and your turning up and watching him the way you did made me suspicious. I couldn't place you. I slipped into your room last night when you were out of it, and it was I who sneaked the little packet from under your pillow. When I opened it and found it wasn't what I was after, I took the first opportunity of returning it to your room.'

'That makes things a little clearer certainly,' said George thoughtfully. 'I seem to have made rather an ass of myself all through.'

'I wouldn't say that, sir. You did uncommon well for a beginner. You say you visited the bathroom this morning and took away what was concealed behind the skirting board?'

'Yes. But it's only a rotten love letter,' said George gloomily. 'Dash it all, I didn't mean to go nosing out the poor fellow's private life.'

'Would you mind letting me see it, sir?'

George took a folded letter from his pocket and passed it to the inspector. The latter unfolded it.

'As you say, sir. But I rather fancy that if you drew lines from one dotted *i* to another, you'd get a different result. Why, bless you, sir, this is a plan of the Portsmouth harbour defences.'

'What?'

'Yes. We've had our eye on the gentleman for some time. But he was too sharp for us. Got a woman to do most of the dirty work.'

'A woman?' said George, in a faint voice. 'What was her name?'

'She goes by a good many, sir. Most usually known as Betty Brighteyes. A remarkably good-looking young woman she is.'

'Betty—Brighteyes,' said George. 'Thank you, Inspector.'

'Excuse me, sir, but you're not looking well.'

'I'm not well. I'm very ill. In fact, I think I'd better take the first train back to town.'

The Inspector looked at his watch.

'That will be a slow train, I'm afraid, sir. Better wait for the express.'

'It doesn't matter,' said George gloomily. 'No train could be slower than the one I came down by yesterday.'

Seated once more in a first-class carriage, George leisurely perused the day's news. Suddenly he sat bolt upright and stared at the sheet in front of him.

'A romantic wedding took place yesterday in London when Lord Roland Gaigh, second son of the Marquis of Axminster, was married to the Grand Duchess Anastasia of Catonia. The ceremony was kept a profound secret. The Grand Duchess has been living in Paris with her uncle since the upheaval in Catonia. She met Lord Roland when he was secretary to the British Embassy in Catonia and their attachment dates from that time.'

'Well, I'm—'

Mr Rowland could not think of anything strong enough to express his feelings. He continued to stare into space. The train stopped at a small station and a lady got in. She sat down opposite him.

'Good-morning, George,' she said sweetly.

'Good heavens!' cried George. 'Elizabeth!'

She smiled at him. She was, if possible, lovelier than ever.

'Look here,' cried George, clutching his head. 'For

God's sake tell me. Are you the Grand Duchess Anastasia, or are you Betty Brighteyes?'

She stared at him.

'I'm not either. I'm Elizabeth Gaigh. I can tell you all about it now. And I've got to apologize too. You see, Roland (that's my brother) has always been in love with Alexa—'

'Meaning the Grand Duchess?'

'Yes, that's what the family call her. Well, as I say, Roland was always in love with her, and she with him. And then the revolution came, and Alexa was in Paris, and they were just going to fix it up when old Stürm, the chancellor, came along and insisted on carrying off Alexa and forcing her to marry Prince Karl, her cousin, a horrid pimply person—'

'I fancy I've met him,' said George.

'Whom she simply hates. And old Prince Usric, her uncle, forbade her to see Roland again. So she ran away to England, and I came up to town and met her, and we wired to Roland who was in Scotland. And just at the very last minute, when we were driving to the Registry Office in a taxi, whom should we meet in another taxi face to face, but old Prince Usric. Of course he followed us, and we were at our wits' end what to do because he'd have made the most fearful scene, and, anyway, he is her guardian. Then I had the brilliant idea of changing places. You can practically see nothing of a girl nowadays but the tip of her nose. I put on Alexa's red hat and brown wrap coat, and she put on my grey. Then we told the taxi to go to Waterloo, and I skipped out there and hurried into the station. Old Osric followed the red hat all right, without a thought for the other occupant of the taxi sitting huddled up inside, but of course it wouldn't do for him to see my face. So I just bolted into your carriage and threw myself on your mercy.'

'I've got that all right,' said George. 'It's the rest of it.'

'I know. That's what I've got to apologize about. I hope you won't be awfully cross. You see, you looked so keen on its being a real mystery—like in books, that I really couldn't resist the temptation. I picked out a rather sinister looking man on the platform and told you to follow him. And then I thrust the parcel on you.'

'Containing a wedding ring.'

'Yes. Alexa and I bought that, because Roland wasn't due to arrive from Scotland until just before the wedding. And of course I knew that by the time I got to London they wouldn't want it—they would have had to use a curtain ring or something.'

'I see,' said George. 'It's like all these things—so simple when you know! Allow me, Elizabeth.'

He stripped off her left glove, and uttered a sigh of relief at the sight of the bare third finger.

'That's all right,' he remarked. 'That ring won't be wasted after all.'

'Oh!' cried Elizabeth; 'but I don't know anthing about you.'

'You know how nice I am,' said George. 'By the way, it has just occurred to me, you are the Lady Elizabeth Gaigh, of course.'

'Oh! George, are you a snob?'

'As a matter of fact, I am, rather. My best dream was one where King George borrowed half a crown from me to see him over the weekend. But I was thinking of my uncle—the one from whom I am estranged. He's a frightful snob. When he knows I'm going to marry you, and that we'll have a title in the family, he'll make me a partner at once!'

'Oh! George, is he very rich?'

'Elizabeth, are you mercenary?'

'Very. I adore spending money. But I was thinking of Father. Five daughters, full of beauty and blue blood. He's just yearning for a rich son-in-law.'

'H'm,' said George. 'It will be one of those marriages made in Heaven and approved on earth. Shall we live at Rowland's Castle? They'd be sure to make me Lord Mayor with you for a wife. Oh! Elizabeth, darling, it's probably contravening the company's by-laws, but I simply must kiss you!'

Greenshaw's Folly

The two men rounded the corner of the shrubbery.

'Well, there you are,' said Raymond West. 'That's it.'

Horace Bindler took a deep, appreciative breath.

'But my dear,' he cried, 'how wonderful.' His voice rose in a high screech of 'sthetic delight, then deepened in reverent awe. 'It's unbelievable. Out of this world! A period piece of the best.'

'I thought you'd like it,' said Raymond West, complacently.

'Like it? My dear——' Words failed Horace. He unbuckled the strap of his camera and got busy. 'This will be one of the gems of my collection,' he said happily. 'I do think, don't you, that it's rather amusing to have a collection of monstrosities? The idea came to me one night seven years ago in my bath. My last real gem was in the Campo Santo at Genoa, but I really think this beats it. What's it called?'

'I haven't the least idea,' said Raymond.

'I suppose it's got a name?'

'It must have. But the fact is that it's never referred to round here as anything but Greenshaw's Folly.'

'Greenshaw being the man who built it?'

'Yes. In eighteen-sixty or seventy or thereabouts. The local success story of the time. Barefoot boy who had risen to immense prosperity. Local opinion is divided as to why he built this house, whether it was sheer exuberance of wealth or whether it was done to impress his creditors. If the latter, it didn't impress them. He either went bankrupt or the next thing to it. Hence the name, Greenshaw's Folly.'

Horace's camera clicked. 'There,' he said in a satisfied voice. 'Remind me to show you No. 310 in my collection. A really incredible marble mantelpiece in the Italian manner.' He added, looking at the house, 'I can't conceive of how Mr Greenshaw thought of it all.'

'Rather obvious in some ways,' said Raymond. 'He had visited the châteaux of the Loire, don't you think? Those turrets. And then, rather unfortunately, he seems to have travelled in the Orient. The influence of the Taj Mahal is unmistakable. I rather like the Moorish wing,' he added, 'and the traces of a Venetian palace.'

'One wonders how he ever got hold of an architect to carry out these ideas.'

Raymond shrugged his shoulders.

'No difficulty about that, I expect,' he said. 'Probably the architect retired with a good income for life while poor old Greenshaw went bankrupt.'

'Could we look at it from the other side?' asked Horace, 'or are we trespassing!'

'We're trespassing all right,' said Raymond, 'but I don't think it will matter.'

He turned towards the corner of the house and Horace skipped after him.

'But who lives here, my dear? Orphans or holiday visitors? It can't be a school. No playing-fields or brisk efficiency.'

'Oh, a Greenshaw lives here still,' said Raymond over his shoulder. 'The house itself didn't go in the crash. Old Greenshaw's son inherited it. He was a bit of a miser and lived here in a corner of it. Never spent a penny. Probably never had a penny to spend. His daughter lives here now. Old lady—very eccentric.'

As he spoke Raymond was congratulating himself on having thought of Greenshaw's Folly as a means of entertaining his guest. These literary critics always professed themselves as longing for a weekend in the country, and were wont to find the country extremely boring when they got there. Tomorrow there would be the Sunday papers, and for today Raymond West congratulated himself on suggesting a visit to Greenshaw's Folly to enrich Horace Bindler's well-known collection of monstrosities.

They turned the corner of the house and came out on a neglected lawn. In one corner of it was a large artificial rockery, and bending over it was a figure at sight of which Horace clutched Raymond delightedly by the arm.

'My dear,' he exclaimed, 'do you see what she's got on? A sprigged print dress. Just like a housemaid—when there were housemaids. One of my most cherished memories is staying at a house in the country when I was quite a boy where a real housemaid called you in the morning, all crackling in a print dress and a cap. Yes, my boy, really—a cap. Muslin with streamers. No, perhaps it was the parlour-maid who had the streamers. But anyway she was a real housemaid and she brought in an enormous brass can of hot water. What an exciting day we're having.'

The figure in the print dress had straightened up and had turned towards them, trowel in hand. She was a sufficiently startling figure. Unkempt locks of iron-grey fell wispily on her shoulders, a straw hat rather like the hats that horses wear in Italy was crammed down on her head. The coloured print dress she wore fell nearly to her ankles. Out of a weatherbeaten, not-too-clean face, shrewd eyes surveyed them appraisingly.

'I must apologize for trespassing, Miss Greenshaw,' said Raymond West, as he advanced towards her, 'but Mr Horace Bindler who is staying with me—'

Horace bowed and removed his hat.

'—is most interested in—er—ancient history and—er—fine buildings.'

Raymond West spoke with the ease of a well-known author who knows that he is a celebrity, that he can venture where other people may not.

Miss Greenshaw looked up at the sprawling exuberance behind her.

'It *is* a fine house,' she said appreciatively. 'My grandfather built it—before my time, of course. He is reported as having said that he wished to astonish the natives.'

'I'll say he did that, ma'am,' said Horace Bindler.

'Mr Bindler is the well-known literary critic,' said Raymond West.

Miss Greenshaw had clearly no reverence for literary critics. She remained unimpressed.

'I consider it,' said Miss Greenshaw, referring to the house, 'as a monument to my grandfather's genius. Silly fools come here, and ask me why I don't sell it and go and live in a flat. What would *I* do in a flat? It's my home and I live in it,' said Miss Greenshaw. 'Always have lived here.' She considered, brooding over the past. 'There were three of us. Laura married the curate. Papa wouldn't give her any money, said clergymen ought to be unworldly. She died, having a baby. Baby died too. Nettie ran away with the riding master. Papa cut her out of his will, of course. Handsome fellow, Harry Fletcher, but no good. Don't think Nettie was happy with him.

Anyway, she didn't live long. They had a son. He writes to me sometimes, but of course he isn't a Greenshaw. I'm the last of the Greenshaws.' She drew up her bent shoulders with a certain pride, and readjusted the rakish angle of the straw hat. Then, turning, she said sharply, 'Yes, Mrs Cresswell, what is it?'

Approaching them from the house was a figure that, seen side by side with Miss Greenshaw, seemed ludicrously dissimilar. Mrs Cresswell had a marvellously dressed head of well-blued hair towering upwards in meticulously arranged curls and rolls. It was as though she had dressed her head to go as a French marquise to a fancy-dress party. The rest of her middle-aged person was dressed in what ought to have been rustling black silk but was actually one of the shinier varieties of black rayon. Although she was not a large woman, she had a well-developed and sumptuous bust. Her voice when she spoke, was unexpectedly deep. She spoke with exquisite diction, only a slight hesitation over words beginning with 'h' and the final pronunciation of them with an exaggerated aspirate gave rise to a suspicion that at some remote period in her youth she might have had trouble over dropping her h's.

'The fish, madam,' said Mrs Cresswell, 'the slice of cod. It has not arrived. I have asked Alfred to go down for it and he refuses to do so.'

Rather unexpectedly, Miss Greenshaw gave a cackle of laughter.

'Refuses, does he?'

'Alfred, madam, has been most disobliging.'

Miss Greenshaw raised two earth-stained fingers to her lips, suddenly produced an ear-splitting whistle and at the same time yelled:

'Alfred. Alfred, come here.'

Round the corner of the house a young man appeared in answer to the summons, carrying a spade in his hand. He had a bold, handsome face and as he drew near he cast an unmistakably malevolent glance towards Mrs Cresswell.

'You wanted me, miss?' he said.

'Yes, Alfred. I hear you've refused to go down for the fish. What about it, eh?'

Alfred spoke in a surly voice.

'I'll go down for it if you wants it, miss. You've only got to say.'

'I do want it. I want it for my supper.'

'Right you are, miss. I'll go right away.'

He threw an insolent glance at Mrs Cresswell, who flushed and murmured below her breath:

'Really! It's unsupportable.'

'Now that I think of it,' said Miss Greenshaw, 'a couple of strange visitors are just what we need aren't they, Mrs Cresswell?'

Mrs Cresswell looked puzzled.

'I'm sorry, madam—'

'For you-know-what,' said Miss Greenshaw, nodding her head. 'Beneficiary to a will mustn't witness it. That's right, isn't it?' She appealed to Raymond West.

'Quite correct,' said Raymond.

'I know enough law to know that,' said Miss Greenshaw. 'And you two are men of standing.'

She flung down her trowel on her weeding-basket.

'Would you mind coming up to the library with me?'

'Delighted,' said Horace eagerly.

She led the way through french windows and through a vast yellow and gold drawing-room with faded brocade on the walls and dust covers arranged over the furniture, then through a large dim hall, up a staircase and into a room on the first floor.

'My grandfather's library,' she announced.

Horace looked round the room with acute pleasure. It was a room, from his point of view, quite full of monstrosities. The heads of sphinxes appeared on the most unlikely pieces of furniture, there was a colossal bronze representing, he thought, Paul and Virginia, and a vast bronze clock with classical motifs of which he longed to take a photograph.

'A fine lot of books,' said Miss Greenshaw.

Raymond was already looking at the books. From what he could see from a cursory glance there was no book here of any real interest or, indeed, any book which appeared to have been read. They were all superbly bound sets of the classics as supplied ninety years ago for furnishing a gentleman's library. Some novels of a bygone period were included. But they too showed little signs of having been read.

Miss Greenshaw was fumbling in the drawers of a vast desk. Finally she pulled out a parchment document.

'My will,' she explained. 'Got to leave your money to someone—or so they say. If I died without a will I suppose that son of a horse-coper would get it. Handsome fellow, Harry Fletcher, but a rogue if there ever was one. Don't see why *his* son should inherit this place. No,' she went on, as though answering some unspoken objection, 'I've made up my mind. I'm leaving it to Cresswell.'

'Your housekeeper?'

'Yes. I've explained it to her. I make a will leaving her all I've got and then I don't need to pay her any wages. Saves me a lot in current expenses, and it keeps her up to the mark. No giving me notice and walking off at any minute. Very la-di-dah and all that, isn't she? But her father was a working plumber in a very small way. *She's* nothing to give herself airs about.'

She had by now unfolded the parchment. Picking up a pen she dipped it in the inkstand and wrote her signature, Katherine Dorothy Greenshaw.

'That's right,' she said. 'You've seen me sign it, and then you two sign it, and that makes it legal.'

She handed the pen to Raymond West. He hesitated a moment, feeling an unexpected repulsion to what he was asked to do. Then he quickly scrawled the well-known signature, for which his morning's mail usually brought at least six demands a day.

Horace took the pen from him and added his own minute signature.

'That's done,' said Miss Greenshaw.

She moved across to the bookcase and stood looking at them uncertainly, then she opened a glass door, took out a book and slipped the folded parchment inside.

'I've my own places for keeping things,' she said.

'*Lady Audley's Secret*,' Raymond West remarked, catching sight of the title as she replaced the book.

Miss Greenshaw gave another cackle of laughter.

'Best-seller in its day,' she remarked. 'Not like your books, eh?'

She gave Raymond a sudden friendly nudge in the ribs. Raymond was rather surprised that she even knew he wrote books. Although Raymond West was quite a name in literature, he could hardly be described as a best-seller. Though softening a little with the advent of middle-age, his books dealt bleakly with the sordid side of life.

'I wonder,' Horace demanded breathlessly, 'if I might just take a photograph of the clock?'

'By all means,' said Miss Greenshaw. 'It came, I believe, from the Paris exhibition.'

'Very probably,' said Horace. He took his picture.

'This room's not been used much since my grandfather's time,' said Miss Greenshaw. 'This desk's full of old diaries of his. Interesting, I should think. I haven't the eyesight to read them myself. I'd like to get them published, but I suppose one would have to work on them a good deal.'

'You could engage someone to do that,' said Raymond West.

'Could I really? It's an idea, you know. I'll think about it.'

Raymond West glanced at his watch.

'We mustn't trespass on your kindness any longer,' he said.

'Pleased to have seen you,' said Miss Greenshaw graciously. 'Thought you were the policeman when I heard you coming round the corner of the house.'

'Why a policeman?' demanded Horace, who never minded asking questions.

Miss Greenshaw responded unexpectedly.

'If you want to know the time, ask a policeman,' she carolled, and with this example of Victorian wit, nudged Horace in the ribs and roared with laughter.

'It's been a wonderful afternoon,' sighed Horace as they walked home. 'Really, that place has everything. The only thing the library needs is a body. Those old-fashioned detective stories about murder in the library—that's just the kind of library I'm sure the authors had in mind.'

'If you want to discuss murder,' said Raymond, 'you must talk to my Aunt Jane.'

'Your Aunt Jane? Do you mean Miss Marple?' He felt a little at a loss.

The charming old-world lady to whom he had been

introduced the night before seemed the last person to be mentioned in connection with murder.

'Oh, yes,' said Raymond. 'Murder is a speciality of hers.'

'But my dear, how intriguing. What do you really mean?'

'I mean just that,' said Raymond. He paraphrased: 'Some commit murder, some get mixed up in murders, others have murder thrust upon them. My Aunt Jane comes into the third category.'

'You are joking.'

'Not in the least. I can refer you to the former Commissioner of Scotland Yard, several Chief Constables and one or two hard-working inspectors of the CID.'

Horace said happily that wonders would never cease. Over the tea table they gave Joan West, Raymond's wife, Lou Oxley her niece, and old Miss Marple, a résumé of the afternoon's happenings, recounting in detail everything that Miss Greenshaw had said to them.

'But I do think,' said Horace, 'that there is something a little *sinister* about the whole set-up. That duchess-like creature, the housekeeper—arsenic, perhaps, in the teapot, now that she knows her mistress has made the will in her favour?'

'Tell us, Aunt Jane,' said Raymond. 'Will there be murder or won't there? What do *you* think?'

'I think,' said Miss Marple, winding up her wool with a rather severe air, 'that you shouldn't joke about these things as much as you do, Raymond. Arsenic is, of course, *quite* a possibility. So easy to obtain. Probably present in the toolshed already in the form of weed killer.'

'Oh, really, darling,' said Joan West, affectionately. 'Wouldn't that be rather too obvious?'

'It's all very well to make a will,' said Raymond, 'I don't suppose really the poor old thing has anything to leave except that awful white elephant of a house, and who would want that?'

'A film company possibly,' said Horace, 'or a hotel or an institution?'

'They'd expect to buy it for a song,' said Raymond, but Miss Marple was shaking her head.

'You know, dear Raymond, I cannot agree with you there. About the money, I mean. The grandfather was evidently one of those lavish spenders who make money easily, but can't keep it. He may have gone broke, as you say, but hardly bankrupt or else his son would not have had the house. Now the son, as is so often the case, was an entirely different character to his father. A miser. A man who saved every penny. I should say that in the course of his lifetime he probably put by a very good sum. This Miss Greenshaw appears to have taken after him, to dislike spending money, that is. Yes, I should think it quite likely that she had quite a good sum tucked away.'

'In that case,' said Joan West, 'I wonder now—what about Lou?'

They looked at Lou as she sat, silent, by the fire.

Lou was Joan West's niece. Her marriage had recently, as she herself put it, come unstuck, leaving her with two young children and a bare sufficiency of money to keep them on.

'I mean,' said Joan, 'if this Miss Greenshaw really wants someone to go through diaries and get a book ready for publication ...'

'It's an idea,' said Raymond.

Lou said in a low voice:

'It's work I could do—and I'd enjoy it.'

'I'll write to her,' said Raymond.

'I wonder,' said Miss Marple thoughtfully, 'what the old lady meant by that remark about a policeman?'

'Oh, it was just a joke.'

'It reminded me,' said Miss Marple, nodding her head vigorously, 'yes, it reminded me very much of Mr Naysmith.'

'Who was Mr Naysmith?' asked Raymond, curiously.

'He kept bees,' said Miss Marple, 'and was very good at doing the acrostics in the Sunday papers. And he liked giving people false impressions just for fun. But sometimes it led to trouble.'

Everybody was silent for a moment, considering Mr Naysmith, but as there did not seem to be any points of resemblance between him and Miss Greenshaw, they decided that dear Aunt Jane was perhaps getting a *little* bit disconnected in her old age.

Horace Bindler went back to London without having collected any more monstrosities and Raymond West wrote a letter to Miss Greenshaw telling her that he knew of a Mrs Louisa Oxley who would be competent to undertake work on the diaries. After a lapse of some days, a letter arrived, written in spidery old-fashioned handwriting, in which Miss Greenshaw declared herself anxious to avail herself of the services of Mrs Oxley, and making an appointment for Mrs Oxley to come and see her.

Lou duly kept the appointment, generous terms were arranged and she started work on the following day.

'I'm awfully grateful to you,' she said to Raymond. 'It will fit in beautifully. I can take the children to school, go on to Greenshaw's Folly and pick them up on my way back. How fantastic the whole set-up is! That old woman has to be seen to be believed.'

On the evening of her first day at work she returned and described her day.

'I've hardly seen the housekeeper,' she said. 'She came in with coffee and biscuits at half past eleven with her mouth pursed up very prunes and prisms, and would hardly speak to me. I think she disapproves deeply of my having been engaged.' She went on, 'It seems there's quite a feud between her and the gardener, Alfred. He's a local boy and fairly lazy, I should imagine, and he and the housekeeper won't speak to each other. Miss Greenshaw said in her rather grand way, "There have always been feuds as far as I can remember between the garden and the house staff. It was so in my grandfather's time. There were three men and a boy in the garden then, and eight maids in the house, but there was always friction."'

On the following day Lou returned with another piece of news.

'Just fancy,' she said, 'I was asked to ring up the nephew this morning.'

'Miss Greenshaw's nephew?'

'Yes. It seems he's an actor playing in the company that's doing a summer season at Boreham on Sea. I rang up the theatre and left a message asking him to lunch tomorrow. Rather fun, really. The old girl didn't want the housekeeper to know. I think Mrs Cresswell has done something that's annoyed her.'

'Tomorrow another instalment of this thrilling serial,' murmured Raymond.

'It's exactly like a serial, isn't it? Reconciliation with the nephew, blood is thicker than water—another will to be made and the old will destroyed.'

'Aunt Jane, you're looking very serious.'

'Was I, my dear? Have you heard any more about the policeman?'

Lou looked bewildered. 'I don't know anything about a policeman.'

'That remark of hers, my dear,' said Miss Marple, 'must have meant *something*.'

Lou arrived at her work the next day in a cheerful mood. She passed through the open front door—the doors and windows of the house were always open. Miss Greenshaw appeared to have no fear of burglars, and was probably justified, as most things in the house weighed several tons and were of no marketable value.

Lou had passed Alfred in the drive. When she first caught sight of him he had been leaning against a tree smoking a cigarette, but as soon as he had caught sight of her he had seized a broom and begun diligently to sweep leaves. An idle young man, she thought, but good looking. His features reminded her of someone. As she passed through the hall on her way upstairs to the library she glanced at the large picture of Nathaniel Greenshaw which presided over the mantelpiece, showing him in the acme of Victorian prosperity, leaning back in a large arm-chair, his hands resting on the gold albert across his capacious stomach. As her glance swept up from the stomach to the face with its heavy jowls, its bushy eyebrows and its flourishing black moustache, the thought occurred to her that Nathaniel Greenshaw must have been handsome as a young man. He had looked, perhaps, a little like Alfred . . .

She went into the library, shut the door behind her, opened her typewriter and got out the diaries from the drawer at the side of the desk. Through the open window she caught a glimpse of Miss Greenshaw in a puce-coloured sprigged print, bending over the rockery, weeding assiduously. They had had two wet days, of which the weeds had taken full advantage.

Lou, a town-bred girl, decided that if she ever had a garden it would never contain a rockery which needed hand weeding. Then she settled down to her work.

When Mrs Cresswell entered the library with the coffee tray at half past eleven, she was clearly in a very bad temper. She banged the tray down on the table, and observed to the universe.

'Company for lunch—and nothing in the house! What am *I* supposed to do, I should like to know? And no sign of Alfred.'

'He was sweeping in the drive when I got here,' Lou offered.

'I dare say. A nice soft job.'

Mrs Cresswell swept out of the room and banged the door behind her. Lou grinned to herself. She wondered what 'the nephew' would be like.

She finished her coffee and settled down to her work again. It was so absorbing that time passed quickly. Nathaniel Greenshaw, when he started to keep a diary, had succumbed to the pleasure of frankness. Trying out a passage relating to the personal charm of a barmaid in the neighbouring town, Lou reflected that a good deal of editing would be necessary.

As she was thinking this, she was startled by a scream from the garden. Jumping up, she ran to the open window. Miss Greenshaw was staggering away from the rockery towards the house. Her hands were clasped to her breast and between them there protruded a feathered shaft that Lou recognized with stupefaction to be the shaft of an arrow.

Miss Greenshaw's head, in its battered straw hat, fell

forward on her breast. She called up to Lou in a failing voice: '... shot ... he shot me ... with an arrow ... get help ...'

Lou rushed to the door. She turned the handle, but the door would not open. It took her a moment or two of futile endeavour to realize that she was locked in. She rushed back to the window.

'I'm locked in.'

Miss Greenshaw, her back towards Lou, and swaying a little on her feet was calling up to the housekeeper at a window farther along.

'Ring police ... telephone ...'

Then, lurching from side to side like a drunkard she disappeared from Lou's view through the window below into the drawing-room. A moment later Lou heard a crash of broken china, a heavy fall, and then silence. Her imagination reconstructed the scene. Miss Greenshaw must have staggered blindly into a small table with a Sèvres teaset on it.

Desperately Lou pounded on the door, calling and shouting. There was no creeper or drain-pipe outside the window that could help her to get out that way.

Tired at last of beating on the door, she returned to the window. From the window of her sitting-room farther along, the housekeeper's head appeared.

'Come and let me out, Mrs Oxley. I'm locked in.'

'So am I.'

'Oh dear, isn't it awful? I've telephoned the police. There's an extension in this room, but what I can't understand, Mrs Oxley, is our being locked in. *I* never heard a key turn, did you?'

'No. I didn't hear anything at all. Oh dear, what shall we do? Perhaps Alfred might hear us.' Lou shouted at the top of her voice, 'Alfred, Alfred.'

'Gone to his dinner as likely as not. What time is it?'

Lou glanced at her watch.

'Twenty-five past twelve.'

'He's not supposed to go until half past, but he sneaks off earlier whenever he can.'

'Do you think—do you think—'

Lou meant to ask 'Do you think she's dead?' but the words stuck in her throat.

There was nothing to do but wait. She sat down on the window-sill. It seemed an eternity before the stolid helmeted figure of a police constable came round the corner of the house. She leant out of the window and he looked up at her, shading his eyes with his hand. When he spoke his voice held reproof.

'What's going on here?' he asked disapprovingly.

From their respective windows, Lou and Mrs Cresswell poured a flood of excited information down on him.

The constable produced a note-book and pencil. 'You ladies ran upstairs and locked yourselves in? Can I have your names, please?'

'No. Somebody else locked us in. Come and let us out.'

The constable said reprovingly, 'All in good time,' and disappeared through the window below.

Once again time seemed infinite. Lou heard the sound of a car arriving, and, after what seemed an hour, but was actually three minutes, first Mrs Cresswell and then Lou, were released by a police sergeant more alert than the original constable.

'Miss Greenshaw?' Lou's voice faltered. 'What— what's happened?'

The sergeant cleared his throat.

'I'm sorry to have to tell you, madam,' he said, 'what

I've already told Mrs Cresswell here. Miss Greenshaw is dead.'

'Murdered,' said Mrs Cresswell. 'That's what it is—murder.'

The sergeant said dubiously:

'Could have been an accident—some country lads shooting with bows and arrows.'

Again there was the sound of a car arriving. The sergeant said:

'That'll be the MO,' and started downstairs.

But it was not the MO. As Lou and Mrs Cresswell came down the stairs a young man stepped hesitatingly through the front door and paused, looking round him with a somewhat bewildered air.

Then, speaking in a pleasant voice that in some way seemed familiar to Lou—perhaps it had a family resemblance to Miss Greenshaw's—he asked:

'Excuse me, does—er—does Miss Greenshaw live here?'

'May I have your name if you please,' said the sergeant advancing upon him.

'Fletcher,' said the young man. 'Nat Fletcher. I'm Miss Greenshaw's nephew, as a matter of fact.'

'Indeed, sir, well—I'm sorry—I'm sure—'

'Has anything happened?' asked Nat Fletcher.

'There's been an—accident—your aunt was shot with an arrow—penetrated the jugular vein—'

Mrs Cresswell spoke hysterically and without her usual refinement:

'Your h'aunt's been murdered, that's what's 'appened. Your h'aunt's been murdered.'

Inspector Welch drew his chair a little nearer to the table and let his gaze wander from one to the other of the four people in the room. It was the evening of the same day. He had called at the Wests' house to take Lou Oxley once more over her statement.

'You are sure of the exact words? *Shot—he shot me—with an arrow—get help?*'

Lou nodded.

'And the time?'

'I looked at my watch a minute or two later—it was then twelve twenty-five.'

'Your watch keeps good time?'

'I looked at the clock as well.'

The inspector turned to Raymond West.

'It appears, sir, that about a week ago you and a Mr Horace Bindler were witnesses to Miss Greenshaw's will?'

Briefly, Raymond recounted the events of the afternoon visit that he and Horace Bindler had paid to Greenshaw's Folly.

'This testimony of yours may be important,' said Welch. 'Miss Greenshaw distinctly told you, did she, that her will was being made in favour of Mrs Cresswell, the housekeeper, that she was not paying Mrs Cresswell any wages in view of the expectations Mrs Cresswell had of profiting by her death?'

'That is what she told me—yes.'

'Would you say that Mrs Cresswell was definitely aware of these facts?'

'I should say undoubtedly. Miss Greenshaw made a reference in my presence to beneficiaries not being able to witness a will and Mrs Cresswell clearly understood what she meant by it. Moreover, Miss Greenshaw herself told me that she had come to this arrangement with Mrs Cresswell.'

'So Mrs Cresswell had reason to believe she was an

interested party. Motive's clear enough in her case, and I dare say she'd be our chief suspect now if it wasn't for the fact that she was securely locked in her room like Mrs Oxley here, and also that Miss Greenshaw definitely said a *man* shot her—'

'She definitely *was* locked in her room?'

'Oh yes. Sergeant Cayley let her out. It's a big old-fashioned lock with a big old-fashioned key. The key was in the lock and there's not a chance that it could have been turned from inside or any hanky-panky of that kind. No, you can take it definitely that Mrs Cresswell was locked inside that room and couldn't get out. And there were no bows and arrows in the room and Miss Greenshaw couldn't in any case have been shot from a window—the angle forbids it—no, Mrs Cresswell's out of it.'

He paused and went on:

'Would you say that Miss Greenshaw, in your opinion, was a practical joker?'

Miss Marple looked up sharply from her corner.

'So the will wasn't in Mrs Cresswell's favour after all?' she said.

Inspector Welch looked over at her in a rather surprised fashion.

'That's a very clever guess of yours, madam,' he said. 'No. Mrs Cresswell isn't named as beneficiary.'

'Just like Mr Naysmith,' said Miss Marple, nodding her head. 'Miss Greenshaw told Mrs Cresswell she was going to leave her everything and so got out of paying her wages; and then she left her money to somebody else. No doubt she was vastly pleased with herself. No wonder she chortled when she put the will away in *Lady Audley's Secret*.'

'It was lucky Mrs Oxley was able to tell us about the

will and where it was put,' said the inspector. 'We might have had a long hunt for it otherwise.'

'A Victorian sense of humour,' murmured Raymond West.

'So she left her money to her nephew after all,' said Lou.

The inspector shook his head.

'No,' he said, 'she didn't leave it to Nat Fletcher. The story goes around here—of course I'm new to the place and I only get the gossip that's second-hand—but it seems that in the old days both Miss Greenshaw and her sister were set on the handsome young riding master, and the sister got him. No, she didn't leave the money to her nephew—' He paused, rubbing his chin, 'She left it to Alfred,' he said.

'Alfred—the gardener?' Joan spoke in a surprised voice.

'Yes, Mrs West. Alfred Pollock.'

'But why?' cried Lou.

Miss Marple coughed and murmured:

'I should imagine, though perhaps I am wrong, that there may have been—what we might call *family* reasons.'

'You could call them that in a way,' agreed the inspector. 'It's quite well known in the village, it seems, that Thomas Pollock, Alfred's grandfather, was one of old Mr Greenshaw's by-blows.'

'Of course,' cried Lou, 'the resemblance! I saw it this morning.'

She remembered how after passing Alfred she had come into the house and looked up at old Greenshaw's portrait.

'I dare say,' said Miss Marple, 'that she thought Alfred Pollock might have a pride in the house, might even want to live in it, whereas her nephew would almost

215

certainly have no use for it whatever and would sell it as soon as he could possibly do so. He's an actor, isn't he? What play exactly is he acting in at present?'

Trust an old lady to wander from the point, thought Inspector Welch, but he replied civilly:

'I believe, madam, they are doing a season of James Barrie's plays.'

'Barrie,' said Miss Marple thoughtfully.

'*What Every Woman Knows*,' said Inspector Welch, and then blushed. 'Name of a play,' he said quickly. 'I'm not much of a theatre-goer myself,' he added, 'but the wife went along and saw it last week. Quite well done, she said it was.'

'Barrie wrote some very charming plays,' said Miss Marple, 'though I must say that when I went with an old friend of mine, General Easterly, to see Barrie's *Little Mary*—' she shook her head sadly, '—neither of us knew where to look.'

The inspector, unacquainted with the play *Little Mary* looked completely fogged. Miss Marple explained:

'When I was a girl, Inspector, nobody ever mentioned the word *stomach*.'

The inspector looked even more at sea. Miss Marple was murmuring titles under her breath.

'*The Admirable Crichton*. Very clever. *Mary Rose*—a charming play. I cried, I remember. *Quality Street* I didn't care for so much. Then there was *A Kiss for Cinderella*. Oh, *of course*.'

Inspector Welch had no time to waste on theatrical discussion. He returned to the matter in hand.

'The question is,' he said, 'did Alfred Pollock know that the old lady had made a will in his favour? Did she tell him?' He added: 'You see—there's an archery club over at Boreham Lovell and *Alfred Pollock's a member*.

He's a very good shot indeed with a bow and arrow.'

'Then isn't your case quite clear?' asked Raymond West. 'It would fit in with the doors being locked on the two women—he'd know just where they were in the house.'

The inspector looked at him. He spoke with deep melancholy.

'He's got an alibi,' said the inspector.

'I always think alibis are definitely suspicious.'

'Maybe, sir,' said Inspector Welch. 'You're talking as a writer.'

'I don't write detective stories,' said Raymond West, horrified at the mere idea.

'Easy enough to say that alibis are suspicious,' went on Inspector Welch, 'but unfortunately we've got to deal with facts.'

He sighed.

'We've got three good suspects,' he said. 'Three people who, as it happened, were very close upon the scene at the time. Yet the odd thing is that it looks as though none of the three could have done it. The housekeeper I've already dealt with—the nephew, Nat Fletcher, at the moment Miss Greenshaw was shot, was a couple of miles away filling up his car at a garage and asking his way—as for Alfred Pollock six people will swear that he entered the Dog and Duck at twenty past twelve and was there for an hour having his usual bread and cheese and beer.'

'Deliberately establishing an alibi,' said Raymond West hopefully.

'Maybe,' said Inspector Welch, 'but if so, he *did* establish it.'

There was a long silence. Then Raymond turned his head to where Miss Marple sat upright and thoughtful.

'It's up to you, Aunt Jane,' he said. 'The inspector's

baffled, the sergeant's baffled, I'm baffled, Joan's baffled, Lou is baffled. But to you, Aunt Jane, it is crystal clear. Am I right?'

'I wouldn't say that, dear,' said Miss Marple, 'not *crystal* clear, and murder, dear Raymond, isn't a game. I don't suppose poor Miss Greenshaw wanted to die, and it was a particularly brutal murder. Very well planned and quite cold blooded. It's not a thing to make *jokes* about!'

'I'm sorry,' said Raymond, abashed. 'I'm not really as callous as I sound. One treats a thing lightly to take away from the—well, the horror of it.'

'That is, I believe, the modern tendency,' said Miss Marple, 'All these wars, and having to joke about funerals. Yes, perhaps I was thoughtless when I said you were callous.'

'It isn't,' said Joan, 'as though we'd known her at all well.'

'That is *very* true,' said Miss Marple. 'You, dear Joan, did not know her at all. I did not know her at all. Raymond gathered an impression of her from one afternoon's conversation. Lou knew her for two days.'

'Come now, Aunt Jane,' said Raymond, 'tell us your views. You don't mind, Inspector?'

'Not at all,' said the inspector politely.

'Well, my dear, it would seem that we have three people who had, or might have thought they had, a motive to kill the old lady. And three quite simple reasons why none of the three could have done so. The housekeeper could not have done so because she was locked in her room and because Miss Greenshaw definitely stated that a *man* shot her. The gardener could not have done it because he was inside the Dog and Duck at the time the murder was committed, the nephew could not have done it because he was still some distance away in his car at the time of the murder.'

'Very clearly put, madam,' said the inspector.

'And since it seems most unlikely that any outsider should have done it, where, then, are we?'

'That's what the inspector wants to know,' said Raymond West.

'One so often looks at a thing the wrong way round,' said Miss Marple apologetically. 'If we can't alter the movements or the position of those three people, then couldn't we perhaps alter the time of the murder?'

'You mean that both my watch and the clock were wrong?' asked Lou.

'No dear,' said Miss Marple, 'I didn't mean that at all. I mean that the murder didn't occur when you thought it occurred.'

'But I *saw* it,' cried Lou.

'Well, what I have been wondering, my dear, was whether you weren't *meant* to see it. I've been asking myself, you know, whether that wasn't the real reason why you were engaged for this job.'

'What *do* you mean, Aunt Jane?'

'Well, dear, it seems odd. Miss Greenshaw did not like spending money, and yet she engaged you and agreed quite willingly to the terms you asked. It seems to me that perhaps you were meant to be there in that library on the first floor, looking out of the window so that you could be the key witness—someone from outside of irreproachable good faith—to fix a definite time and place for the murder.'

'But you can't mean,' said Lou, incredulously, 'that Miss Greenshaw *intended* to be murdered.'

'What I mean, dear,' said Miss Marple, 'is that you didn't really know Miss Greenshaw. There's no real reason, is there, why the Miss Greenshaw you saw when you went up to the house should be the same Miss Greenshaw that Raymond saw a few days earlier? Oh, yes, I know,' she went on, to prevent Lou's reply, 'she was wearing the peculiar old-fashioned print dress and the strange straw hat, and had unkempt hair. She corresponded exactly to the description Raymond gave us last weekend. But those two women, you know, were much of an age and height and size. The housekeeper, I mean, and Miss Greenshaw.'

'But the housekeeper is fat!' Lou exclaimed. 'She's got an enormous bosom.'

Miss Marple coughed.

'But my dear, surely, nowadays I have seen—er— them myself in shops most indelicately displayed. It is very easy for anyone to have a—a bust—of *any* size and dimension.'

'What are you trying to say?' demanded Raymond.

'I was just thinking, dear, that during the two or three days Lou was working there, one woman could have played the two parts. You said yourself, Lou, that you hardly saw the housekeeper, except for the one moment in the morning when she brought you in the tray with coffee. One sees those clever artists on the stage coming in as different characters with only a minute or two to spare, and I am sure the change could have been effected quite easily. That marquise head-dress could be just a wig slipped on and off.'

'Aunt Jane! Do you mean that Miss Greenshaw was dead before I started work there?'

'Not dead. Kept under drugs, I should say. A very easy job for an unscrupulous woman like the house-keeper to do. Then she made the arrangements with you and got you to telephone to the nephew to ask him

220

to lunch at a definite time. The only person who would have known that this Miss Greenshaw was *not* Miss Greenshaw would have been Alfred. And if you remember, the first two days you were working there it was wet, and Miss Greenshaw stayed in the house. Alfred never came into the house because of his feud with the housekeeper. And on the last morning Alfred was in the drive, while Miss Greenshaw was working on the rockery—I'd like to have a look at that rockery.'

'Do you mean it was Mrs Cresswell who killed Miss Greenshaw?'

'I think that after bringing you your coffee, the woman locked the door on you as she went out, carried the unconscious Miss Greenshaw down to the drawing-room, then assumed her "Miss Greenshaw" disguise and went out to work on the rockery where you could see her from the window. In due course she screamed and came staggering to the house clutching an arrow as though it had penetrated her throat. She called for help and was careful to say "*he* shot me" so as to remove suspicion from the housekeeper. She also called up to the housekeeper's window as though she saw her there. Then, once inside the drawing-room, she threw over a table with porcelain on it—and ran quickly upstairs, put on her marquise wig and was able a few moments later to lean her head out of the window and tell you that she, too, was locked in.'

'But she *was* locked in,' said Lou.

'I know. That is where the policeman comes in.'

'What policeman?'

'Exactly—what policeman? I wonder, Inspector, if you would mind telling me how and when *you* arrived on the scene?'

The inspector looked a little puzzled.

'At twelve twenty-nine we received a telephone call from Mrs Cresswell, housekeeper to Miss Greenshaw, stating that her mistress had been shot. Sergeant Cayley and myself went out there at once in a car and arrived at the house at twelve thirty-five. We found Miss Greenshaw dead and the two ladies locked in their rooms.'

'So, you see, my dear,' said Miss Marple to Lou. 'The police constable *you* saw wasn't a real police constable. You never thought of him again—one doesn't—one just accepts one more uniform as part of the law.'

'But who—why?'

'As to who—well, if they are playing *A Kiss for Cinderella*, a policeman is the principal character. Nat Fletcher would only have to help himself to the costume he wears on the stage. He'd ask his way at a garage being careful to call attention to the time—twelve twenty-five, then drive on quickly, leave his car round a corner, slip on his police uniform and do his "act".'

'But why?—why?'

'*Someone* had to lock the housekeeper's door on the outside, and someone had to drive the arrow through Miss Greenshaw's throat. You can stab anyone with an arrow just as well as by shooting it—but it needs force.'

'You mean they were both in it?'

'Oh yes, I think so. Mother and son as likely as not.'

'But Miss Greenshaw's sister died long ago.'

'Yes, but I've no doubt Mr Fletcher married again. He sounds the sort of man who would, and I think it possible that the child died too, and that this so-called nephew was the second wife's child, and not really a relation at all. The woman got a post as housekeeper and spied out the land. Then he wrote as her nephew and proposed to call upon her—he may have made some joking reference to coming in his policeman's uniform—

or asked her over to see the play. But I think she suspected the truth and refused to see him. He would have been her heir if she had died without making a will—but of course once she had made a will in the housekeeper's favour (as they thought) then it was clear sailing.'

'But why use an arrow?' objected Joan. 'So very far fetched.'

'Not far fetched at all, dear. Alfred belonged to an archery club—Alfred was meant to take the blame. The fact that he was in the pub as early as twelve twenty was most unfortunate from their point of view. He always left a little before his proper time and that would have been just right—' she shook her head. 'It really seems all wrong—morally, I mean, that Alfred's laziness should have saved his life.'

The inspector cleared his throat.

'Well, madam, these suggestions of yours are very interesting. I shall have, of course, to investigate—'

Miss Marple and Raymond West stood by the rockery and looked down at that gardening basket full of dying vegetation.

Miss Marple murmured:

'Alyssum, saxifrage, cytisus, thimble campanula ... Yes, that's all the proof *I* need. Whoever was weeding here yesterday morning was no gardener—she pulled up plants as well as weeds. So now I *know* I'm right. Thank you, dear Raymond, for bringing me here. I wanted to see the place for myself.'

She and Raymond both looked up at the outrageous pile of Greenshaw's Folly.

A cough made them turn. A handsome young man was also looking at the house.

'Plaguey big place,' he said. 'Too big for nowadays—

or so they say. I dunno about that. If I won a football pool and made a lot of money, that's the kind of house I'd like to build.'

He smiled bashfully at them.

'Reckon I can say so now—that there house was built by my great-grandfather,' said Alfred Pollock. 'And a fine house it is, for all they call it Greenshaw's Folly!'

BIBLIOGRAPHY

Agatha Christie's short stories typically appeared first in magazines and then in her short story books, which tended to be different collections in the UK and the US. This list attempts to catalogue the first publication of each, and gives alternative story titles when used.

The Gunman

Excerpted from *An Autobiography* (1977).

The Market Basing Mystery

First published in the UK in *The Sketch* No. 1603, 17 October 1923, and in the US in *Blue Book Magazine* Vol. 41, No. 1, May 1925. Reprinted in *Poirot's Early Cases* (UK, 1974) and *The Under Dog* (US, 1951).

The Case of the Missing Lady

First published in the UK in *The Sketch* No. 1655, 15 October 1924. Reprinted in *Partners in Crime* (1929).

The Herb of Death

First published in the UK in *Storyteller* Vol. 46, No. 275, March 1930. Reprinted in *The Thirteen Problems* (UK, 1932) aka *The Tuesday Night Club* (US, 1933).

How Does Your Garden Grow?

First published in the US in *Ladies' Home Journal* Vol. 52, No. 6, June 1935, and in the UK in *The Strand* No. 536, August 1935. Reprinted in *The Regatta Mystery* (US, 1939) and *Poirot's Early Cases* (UK, 1974).

Swan Song

First published in the UK in *Grand Magazine* No. 259, September 1926. Reprinted in *The Listerdale Mystery* (UK, 1934) and *The Golden Ball* (US, 1971).

Miss Marple Tells a Story

First published in the UK as 'Behind Closed Doors' in *Home Journal*, 25 May 1935. Reprinted in *The Regatta Mystery* (US, 1939) and *Miss Marple's Final Cases* (UK, 1979).

Have You Got Everything You Want?

First published in the US in *Cosmopolitan*, April 1933, and in the UK as 'On the Orient Express' in *Nash's Pall Mall* Vol. 91, No. 481, June 1933. Reprinted in *Parker Pyne Investigates* (UK, 1934) and *Mr Parker Pyne, Detective* (US, 1946).

The Jewel Robbery at the Grand Metropolitan

First published in the UK as 'The Curious Disappearance of the Opalsen Pearls' in *The Sketch* No. 1572, 14 March 1923. First printed in the US as 'Mrs Opalsen's Pearls' in *Blue Book Magazine* Vol. 37, No. 6. Reprinted in *Poirot Investigates* (UK, 1924; US, 1925).

Ingots of Gold

First published in the UK in *Royal Magazine* No. 352, February 1928, and in the US as 'Solving Six and the Golden Grave' in *Detective Story Magazine*, 16 June 1928. Reprinted in *The Thirteen Problems* (UK, 1932) aka *The Tuesday Night Club* (US, 1933).

The Soul of the Croupier

First published in the US in *Flynn's Weekly* Vol. 19, No. 5, 13 November 1926, and in the UK as 'The Magic of Mr Quin No. 2: The Soul of the Croupier' in *Storyteller* No. 237, January 1927. Reprinted in *The Mysterious Mr Quin* (1930).

The Girl in the Train

First published in the UK in *Grand Magazine* No. 228, February 1924. Reprinted in *The Listerdale Mystery* (UK, 1934) and *The Golden Ball* (US, 1971).

Greenshaw's Folly

First published in the UK in the *Daily Mail*, 3–7 December 1956. Reprinted in *The Adventure of the Christmas Pudding* (UK, 1960) and *Double Sin* (US, 1961).